A Summer Scandal

Seasons of Romance, Volume 3

Meg Osborne

Published by Meg Osborne, 2023.

This is a work of fiction. Similarities to real people, places, or events are entirely coincidental.

A SUMMER SCANDAL

First edition. June 5, 2023.

Copyright © 2023 Meg Osborne.

ISBN: 979-8223088295

Written by Meg Osborne.

Chapter One

"I am surprised you are so eager to go to London!" Mr Edmund Gale announced to his oldest friend and soon-to-be bride.

"I am surprised you are so eager *not* to!" Juliet Turner retorted, turning them almost subconsciously away from the path that would lead most directly from her home to his and insisting upon their taking a little more time together before being forced to part. It was not entirely subconscious, for she knew with some certainty that Edmund's mother was at home and that lady had never been especially fond of Juliet, never more so now that she had ensnared Mrs Gale's only son to matrimony. Juliet smiled, unable to resist the humour in the thought that she was capable of *ensnaring* or otherwise persuading Edmund Gale to do anything other than what he wanted.

"Oh, I see how it is." He paused at a stile, offering his hand to his companion in a silent show of chivalry. Juliet eschewed his help, hoisting up her skirts with one hand and using the other to scramble quite easily over the stile she had climbed more times than she could count. Edward snorted and followed her, jogging a little to close the space between them.

"You intend me to list every reason why we ought *not* go to London, in the face of your determined position for going, and at the last moment, when I have almost exhausted myself in thinking, you will nod your head and beam at me and declare that staying at home is quite clearly a sensible idea, never once disclosing that it was your plan all along. Do not forget, Juliet, I know you too well to be so easily manipulated!"

"Manipulated?" Juliet sniffed, although there was a small fragment of truth to Edmund's words. She shook her head. "I should never seek to manipulate you. If I did not wish to go to London I should say so and not feel the need to flatter you into making the right decision."

"You might flatter me a little," Edmund put in, reaching out at the last moment to steady Juliet, who had missed her footing and pitched forward. "Heaven knows I am in need of it."

"In need of it?" Juliet shot him a mischievous smile that served as both an encouragement and a thank you. "Since when have you needed flattery?"

"My dearest Juliet, since I began my campaign in earnest to win your heart." He grew serious for a moment, and Juliet felt her smile slip. They had slowed in their progress until they were barely walking at all.

"You were reticent to the last, leaving me to wonder by the hour whether I stood even the slightest chance of securing your affections." He rubbed his nose. "It is hard on a fellow to live in such uncertainty. And now I have it -" He had somehow caught hold of her hand and squeezed it warmly between both of his, before pressing the ghost of a kiss to her palm and releasing it. "My mother refuses to speak to me. Worse still, she scarcely acknowledges my existence!"

Juliet's fingers folded over the spot on her palm that still burned with the fleeting touch of his lips and tried to hide the smile that Edmund's affections evoked. She turned to scan the horizon, her eyes arrested by the sight of a tall figure striding towards them along the very path that they were poised to take.

"How fortunate, then, that you do not have to face her alone!"

Edmund looked at her, thinking, for a moment, that she volunteered to accompany him, and poised to play chivalry a second time in as many minutes. If Mrs Gale's wrath was hard to bear for him, he certainly would not seek to subject his fiancée to it, knowing only too well that Juliet would either blow up in the face of Mrs Gale's cruelty or freeze. He was not sure which outcome he would prefer. He followed her gaze and his stance changed.

"Good afternoon, Mr Weston!" Juliet called, waving at Edmund's friend who had lately become their neighbour, as his stay at Northridge Place extended ever longer.

"Good afternoon, Miss Turner." Nash Weston dropped in a theatrical bow, and as he straightened his smile grew. "You save me a journey," he continued, as he drew level with the pair, and clapped Edmund on the shoulder warmly and a little too energetically to be entirely painless. "I was sent in search of you."

"And see, you have found me," Edmund grumbled, moving closer to Juliet again and offering her his arm. She took it but did not look away from the two gentlemen. She was not insensible of the growing resentment Edmund felt towards his friend and it seemed that news of their engagement, and the ensuing estrangement between himself and his mother, had not served to remedy the problem.

If anything, Juliet thought, *Nash's presence makes it worse!*

Mrs Gale had taken to favouring Mr Weston over her own son, making a great show of taking interest in his affairs, despatching him on errands that ordinarily would have fallen to Edmund and generally seeking to divide the entire household further.

Juliet squeezed Edmund's arm swiftly and secretly, scarcely noticeable to any but the two of them. *Courage*, she silently urged him. *Do not blame your friend for your mother's partiality.*

Juliet knew Nash Weston well and liked him, perhaps best of all of Edmund's *London friends* and she knew that Edmund would bear this current trial all the better with a friend to confide in. *A friend who is not me*, she thought, knowing that Edmund curbed the worst of his temper around her, and whilst there was little the pair concealed from one another, she could not expect a complete show of vulnerability from her cheery, good-natured fiancé.

"Well, Nash, I suppose we ought to return home." He turned to drop a light kiss on Juliet's cheek. "You need not come any further, Juliet, unless you wish to?"

There was the tiniest note of pleading in his voice, and Juliet relented almost immediately. She might have no personal desire to call upon Mrs Gale, but she had faced worse lions on behalf of those she loved, and she would not send Edmund into battle alone.

"I think perhaps I shall," she said, lifting her chin and forcing a smile she hoped was convincing onto her face. "It is far too long since I last called on your mother, and I know *my* mother wished to send her best regards. Who better to bring them than me?"

Edmund visibly brightened and straightened, growing several inches with the buoyancy of love and the comfort of her presence.

"A fine plan!" Nash declared, clapping his hands approvingly. "Now, Miss Turner, if you don't mind, I shall let you pair go on without me. I had hoped to find you at home." He glanced from Edmund to Juliet. "Ah, that is, *your* home." He patted his chest, indicating the pocket of his coat. "I have a book to return to your father, so I shall continue with that task, if you do not mind it, and exchange it for the next in the series, which he had promised to me upon my finishing this."

"Tell Mama I have gone to call at Northridge, then, won't you?" Juliet asked, already turning Edmund back towards the path he had unconsciously veered away from. "And Edmund, you may continue to impress upon me all that is dreadful abut London, and why we should not even countenance going there..."

Edmund grinned, pleased to return to their easy banter of a few moments before, and already summoning the best of his arguments for deployment so he did not see the way Nash's face fell. To be sure, it was scarcely a *fall* merely a shadow, resting fleetingly over the elegant, gentlemanly features before flitting away again but Juliet noticed it and she stored it away to consider later. Few things seemed to upset Edmund's friend, but the mention of London had, and Juliet's inquisitive mind already begged to know why.

LOUISA TURNER HAD NEVER been very fond of reading. Occasionally, she could manage to make it through a novel or two belonging to her sister, but her tastes trended towards the thrilling and scandalous rather more than Juliet would permit. However, she had observed the benefit of having a book to hand, for it afforded one the opportunity to appear busy when one was, in truth, lolling by the window and watching for visitors. They were in anticipation of no callers that afternoon, but Louisa was desperate for some company beyond that of her sisters and had cause to hope that maybe, just maybe, she could bring about a visit merely by wishing it.

"Are you enjoying your book, Louisa?"

Mr Turner's droll voice broke through Louisa's thoughts and she flinched, jumping so dramatically that her book flew to the floor with a loud thump. She glared accusingly at her father, who merely smiled as if he saw through her ruse and returned his attention to his singular card game.

The Turner parlour was quiet. Without Juliet and Edmund around, each of its occupants fell to their own silent, self-contained amusements. Bess was writing a letter, with as contented a smile as she had ever worn, resting on her face. Ordinarily, Louisa might have begged her to play for them, but she was reluctant to call her from a task she was so engaged in.

A change seemed to have swept over Louisa's sister since the announcement of her engagement to an eminent pianist, and Louisa felt certain she would not respond to her bossing with anything like the meekness that had heretofore been a hallmark of their relationship. She sighed, tugging absentmindedly at one of her golden curls and wondering why, of all her sisters, *she* should be the one left alone, with nary a suitor nor an excitement on the horizon of her short, simple life.

It was no surprise that Maddy should marry, she mused, reaching down to retrieve her book and thinking over the year to date, marvelling at how many great changes had befallen the small Turner family in the spate of only a few months. *She is the eldest, and it was surely only a matter of time. I oughtn't to begrudge Bess, either.* It had been a shock to all the family that quiet, homely Bess should secure for herself a suitor, and one as famed as Christopher Cluett, but one glance at the pair together and it was clear that they were perfect for one another, each so enamoured with music that their life promised to be one symphony after another. *Bess will get to travel all over Europe accompanying him,* Louisa thought, with a pout she could not quite conceal, even though she did not begrudge Bess her happiness. *And I shall be left here all alone, with nothing to do and no-one to see!* If any of the sisters were destined to stay at home, Louisa had never once considered the possibility that it might be her.

Even Juliet is engaged! This was both surprising and not, for Juliet and Edmund had been destined to marry for as long as anyone had known them. *And they suit one another perfectly!* Louisa thought, with a sly smile. *They shall aggravate each other excessively all their lives, and leave the rest of us in peace!* She had a somewhat fractious relationship with Juliet, for they were both swift-tempered and frayed one another's nerves almost beyond bearing. Edmund, too, was an annoying brother in all but name. She could not count that a change worthy of note. But still, it left one undeniable fact to poke at Louisa's contentment. She, the most beautiful and charming of all her sisters, was left without prospects or proposals, while all her sisters' futures were assured. *It isn't fair!*

She was poised on the edge of melancholy and wondered if even a book should be enough to shield her from her parents' scrutiny, for Mrs Turner had laid down her sewing and was peering at her youngest daughter with an air of concern. Before Louisa could say or do anything, though, a knock at the window startled her and she glanced up, wiping every trace of tears from her large blue eyes as she saw the smiling, handsome face of Nash Weston.

"Oh!" she squawked, scrambling off her perch and to her feet, pinching colour into her cheeks and affixing a smile just in time for the parlour door to open. Nash burst in ahead of the servant sent to introduce him.

"Good afternoon, dearest Turners!" He beamed around the room, but his eyes rested at last and at length, on Louisa. "Miss Louisa, you looked quite charming bent over your book in the window just now. It was almost a shame to disturb you!"

He slid a slim volume from his pocket and strode over to Mr Turner. "I come to return a book of my own, and thank you for the lend of it."

Mr Turner nodded but did not look up from his cards, and not for the first time, Louisa felt a strange, fleeting sensation that her father did not greatly approve of their newest neighbour. She shook off the feeling, bidding Nash join her in sitting down near enough to her mother and Bess to be proper but far enough away that they might converse as freely as they wished without too great a fear of being overheard.

"I was just saying to Bess that it has been so long since we last saw you!" she cooed, ducking her head a little, and grateful that she had afforded her curls a little more attention that morning.

"It is but a day or two at most," Nash countered, with a wide smile. "But I am grateful to have been so missed! I suppose I cannot hope for such a blessing when you all remove to London."

An icy breeze seemed to blow through the parlour, and Louisa glared at Bess, who bent even closer over her work and pretended not to notice.

"What did I say?" Nash asked, concealing his words behind his hand so that only Louisa might hear them.

"We are not all going to London!" Louisa declared, bristling at the selfishness of certain of her sisters. "At the moment I am not even sure we shall go at all!"

"Louisa." On any other afternoon, Mr Turner's one-word warning would have been enough to quell Louisa from any further complaint, but she was in an especially thorny mood that afternoon, and lacking a good sparring partner in Juliet, she turned her disappointment over to Nash, certain that he would take her side. She felt, just then, that she might benefit from a little sympathy from so handsome a gentleman.

"Bess prefers to stay here because she does not wish to be separated from Mr Cluett!" she wailed. "So *I* must be forced to forego the visit as well, and I did so *long* to see London!"

"London is not so very spectacular, Miss Louisa," Nash said, shifting his weight in his seat and making a show of examining his fingernails. "You should enjoy staying here with your sister far better, I wager."

"I wager *not*!" Louisa seethed, disproportionately annoyed that her concerns could be so easily overlooked. "And I am sure

London is not *so very spectacular* to gentlemen that spend half their time there..."

Nash's head snapped up and he smiled at her, driven to penance.

"Quite so," he said, with a sigh. "Forgive me. But why must you all stay? Surely you can travel with Juliet and Edmund. You sister shall want a companion, won't she?"

Louisa bit her lip. She had had this very suggestion already thrust upon her by her mother and had felt her inadequacy to the task. Her relationship with Juliet was fraught, and if the visit to London was to be as stressful as Juliet expected it to be, she could not imagine that she would be the person her bad-tempered sister would seek to invite.

Nash somehow seemed to sense this without her explaining it, for he leant a little closer, his elbow knocking hers in a way that was surely not accidental.

"I am sure you could make yourself quite agreeable and helpful to Miss Turner, such that she would be only too happy to take you with her. T'would not be so very hard, would it?"

Louisa gazed into his dark, dreamy eyes and felt as if the decision was already half-made. He would be returning to London as well, and perhaps he wished her to go with him! He could not say as much, of course, but this was as close an invitation as she would get.

She nodded, never once breaking their gaze, and her smile grew. *Well,* she reasoned. *If suitors do not befall a young lady in her home town, she must seek them abroad...even if that means following one to London!*

Chapter Two

Nash's mood, buoyed by a quarter-hour in the company of happy people, began to sink as he drew within sight of Northridge Place. He slowed his pace, dragging his heels with every step he took towards home. *Home.* He smiled grimly at the thought. He was outstaying his welcome, he knew that. Edmund was not subtle in his opinion that his friend might consider a return to his *actual* home, although these hints had lessened in quantity in recent days.

Doubtless, he is too consumed with thoughts of love, Nash thought, his smile slipping into a grimace. Edmund Gale must be one of the most fortunate men alive! He was wealthy and well-thought-of, and, imbued with the independence only wealth could bring, free to marry precisely as he had chosen. And he had chosen pretty, clever Juliet Turner. There were worse fates.

Nash recalled, with a shudder, the parade of wealthy wallflowers - none of them particularly pretty or even very young - his Aunt Reed had paraded before him when last he visited her. This was his true reason for avoiding London, for remaining long past his due at Northridge and choosing to ignore any hints his friend made about returning. Sooner or later, he must choose, and if he cared to see a penny of his inheritance, he must make the same choice as his aunt. She was growing weary of Nash's merry ways as she tired of his friends, but even they no longer offered him the comfort and support they might once have done. Heatherington was married, Finch in business, and now even Edmund had bid farewell to bachelorhood. Nash was all that was left, and if he did not settle soon - settle *well* - his line of credit with his aunt would dry up entirely. It was all but gone now, and that would perhaps be reason enough to risk returning to London.

Reaching the driveway, Nash paused, chewing on his lip. If he pitched it just right then perhaps a short visit might be enough to stretch her patience another six months or so. Just long enough until...until...

Nash kicked at a piece of gravel in frustration, before recalling where he stood and hurrying to reassert control over himself, lest he was spied in any way discomforted.

It is a cruelty to make a man contort himself for the pleasure of others. What must it be like to have wealth enough to make one's own decision, and not forever be beholden to others for support? He scowled as he crossed the threshold, envying Edmund more than his engagement at that moment. Northridge was a splendid estate and did not even encapsulate the whole of the wealth that rested on his handsome friend's broad shoulders. He was free to do precisely as he pleased and suffer no consequences...

"Is that you, Mr Weston?"

Nash paused, his scowl melting into a smile that was neither kind nor becoming. Perhaps Edmund was not free of *all* consequences...

"It is, Mrs Gale!" he called, letting his voice ring with music and merriment.

"Ah, how well you look!" She greeted him with a smile as he turned the corner into the opulent parlour. He almost shivered, although the room was temperate. The feel of the place was so unlike the comfortable Turners' that he was not surprised to see Edmund wearing a scowl, and Juliet eyeing the door with a thinly disguised eagerness to escape through it.

Striding forward as if a long-lost heir to this particular parlour, Nash paused before Mrs Gale's chair and bowed, stiff and formal but undeniably pleasing to the recipient, who coloured prettily at this display of manners, and waved him to a seat on her left.

"You were a long time," Edmund remarked, coolly.

"Was I?" Nash shrugged a shoulder, with a self-deprecating smile. "I did not mean to be. I fell to talking, I suppose. T'would have been rude to go all that way and not stop a spell and speak to the neighbours."

"Yes, Miss Turner said you had called at her house," Mrs Gale remarked, her gaze flickering to Juliet and back to Nash, deliberately ignoring her son. "They are all well, I trust?"

"Juliet has just told you they are, Mama," Edmund remarked, stopped mid-comment by Juliet, who laid a calming hand on his arm.

"I should like to hear Mr Weston's opinion, though. Perhaps disaster has befallen them in the hour since I last saw them." Juliet laughed, evidently attempting to lighten the atmosphere and failing, her laughter trailing off into nothing and an awkward silence settling over the quartet before she spoke again.

"And were they well? Tell me, had Bess finished her letter yet?"

"Almost," Nash offered, pleased to throw a lifeline to Juliet in a way he might not have chosen to do for her beau. He liked Juliet Turner as he was fond of all the Turners and envied Edmund their friendship too, in addition to all his other virtues. "Very busy with it she was, too."

In truth, he could recall nothing of the letter nor its writer, for Bess had been too quiet to garner much notice of his even before the surprising news of her engagement to the equally quiet maestro from Castleford.

Even Mrs Gale could find nothing bad to say about the shy, musical Miss Elizabeth and strove instead to turn the conversation in an entirely new direction by clearing her throat.

"Mr Weston, I believe a letter arrived for you this afternoon, I do not suppose you have seen it yet." She inclined her head towards the mantel, and when Nash followed her gaze he saw a folded square wedged neatly beneath an ornate carriage clock. He nodded, but when she did not immediately speak again, realised there would be no easy dismissal of this observation without him acting on it. He stood, crossing the elegant parlour, and snatching up the note. A perfunctory glance at the address identified the sender, although Nash was hardly surprised. He had ignored his aunt's previous two letters. He was long overdue a third.

"Won't you read it?" Mrs Gale's voice grew low and teasing. "Or, perhaps, you are a keeper of secrets. We shall not enquire -"

"It is merely a note from my aunt, Mrs Gale," Nash said, shortly, in hopes of bringing this line of enquiry to a swift close. This answer did nothing but encourage her more, though, for he had forgotten that Mrs Gale and his aunt were a little acquainted.

"Oh, indeed! How is Mrs Reed? You will be returning to see her before long, I do not doubt."

Nash smiled, tightly, deflecting this attention by drawing Edmund back into the fray.

"I daresay I shall, Madam, when we all return to London. Did Miss Turner succeed in persuading you to fix a date for your journey, Ed?"

Edmund swallowed a groan and his mother's eyes narrowed, turning her interrogatory powers on him, and allowing Nash a moment to break the seal of his letter and sweep its contents in a glance, grimacing and refolding the note before sliding it safely into his sleeve and out of sight.

"You are not eager to go to London?" Mrs Gale demanded. "No, do not pepper me with excuses. If you are determined to marry, you simply must visit London beforehand. There are preparations to be made that can only be done there. And in any case," she sniffed, dismissing Edmund's comments before he could make one. "*I* should like to go to London. I suppose you have not spared a thought for my wishes, though, now that your course is set..."

"I SHALL MISS YOU SO!"

Juliet was taking a turn about the Hodges' parlour with her elder sister as an unfortunate turn in the weather ensured everyone stayed under cover.

"Miss me! You shall scarcely have the time to miss me!" Maddy laughed. She tweaked one of her sister's curls good-naturedly. "And it is not as if we are to be parted *forever*! Your visit to London will be but a short one, and then you shall come back here for the wedding."

Juliet nodded, her eyes darting towards one corner of the parlour, where her brother-in-law sat with his father and Mr Turner, their heads bent over a card game. The low rumble of voices betrayed their conversation, and their attention to their cards took a slow second to their discussion.

"It will be lovely to have another wedding to attend!" Maddy repeated, with a contented sigh. "And to know that you will be making your home so close by!"

Juliet shot her sister an accusing glance.

"I do not recall you being so concerned with remaining close by when *you* were the one getting married!"

Maddy pursed her lips, but could only remain silent for a moment before dissolving in giggles.

"Very true. But I have nursed a secret wish to see you and Edmund married for almost as long as I can remember. I am pleased you have finally come to your senses and accepted him! How happy you shall be, tormenting each other from morning and night, as long as you both shall live...ouch!"

Maddy squealed as Juliet poked her sister sharply in the ribs.

"I'd think you might let our last meeting pass without resorting to teasing me!" She pouted but again could maintain the pose for only a moment. "And I should not need to *torment* Edmund if he would learn to behave himself!"

"Like you?" Maddy shook her head, smiling at the thought of her harum-scarum sister being forced to take on the role of a respectable society bride. "Perhaps it is best for all concerned that your visit to London will be a short one. You have never been a great one for society, Jules."

"Society has never been a great one for *me*," Juliet retorted. "If we were permitted to speak as we pleased, to whom we pleased, then things would go far easier. Why must I always be forced to sit with other young ladies who have nothing but air between their ears, discussing the merits of Belgian lace over French? I have a brain, and I shouldn't be prevented from using it."

"As if Edmund has ever succeeded in keeping you from thinking for yourself!" Maddy scoffed. "He has never tried!"

"He knows better." Juliet's tone softened, and she prayed her sister did not notice the warmth that rushed into her cheeks as she thought with fondness of her fiancé. Edmund *was* good, far more than she deserved in a husband. She had tried to persuade him to choose another, but he had been steadfast in his affections, and she knew that they would be happy together, no matter how her sister teased.

"Now, tell me what you plan to do in London," Maddy pressed, turning her sister towards the window and stopping to look out at the gardens, which were a little damp and overcast from the rain, but still sparklingly green. "You shall purchase your trousseau of course."

"Yes." Juliet rolled her eyes. "And oh, how Mama rejoices over it. She has insisted upon Louisa coming with us, for, and I quote, *I wish to have one daughter with taste to assist me!*" Juliet frowned. "I dread to think how they shall primp and preen and dress me up for the occasion. Edmund shall hardly recognise me!"

"I shall put a stop to too much *preening*," Maddy promised, with a solemn smile. "You shall look like my Juliet and none other, although the very best version of yourself, in honour of the day. The wedding will be at Northridge?"

"Mmm-hmmm." Juliet nodded, although she could not be entirely sure of her answer. She knew that Edmund cared little where they were married, and in all honesty neither did she. It was Mrs Gale who was the sticking point. She refused to be drawn on the matter of the wedding itself, and Juliet nursed a secret suspicion that she still hoped it would be somehow delayed, or disposed of entirely. She rubbed at an invisible spot of ink on her fingertip, wondering if this trip to London could spell disaster for the happy couple. Edmund knew her and loved her, she did not deny that, but she was also firmly part of his life at home. He had rarely, if ever, seen her in London, amongst his elegant society friends. One glimpse of her there, now, and would Edmund rethink his commitment?

"The parish church is very pretty too," Maddy conceded, noticing her sister's reticence and hoping to overcome it. "And Reverend Worthy will certainly ensure the church is arrayed to its greatest advantage on such a day." She glanced out of the window and sighed. "Hopefully the weather will comply, too. It is supposed to be summer!"

"We cannot have sunshine all our days, Maddy, dear!" Mr Hodge remarked, from his corner, betraying that the gentlemen were not quite so engaged in their cards or their conversation as they had appeared to be.

"Well, Juliet." Mr Turner stood, shaking hands with his friends and turning towards his daughters with a warm smile. "We had better beat a return to home. Your Mama was quite determined she could spare us for only a short time. Maddy, dear, we shall see you upon our return, which will not be above a week or two."

"Give my love to Aunt and Uncle, Papa," Maddy said, turning her cheek so that her father could press a dry kiss against it. She squeezed Juliet's hand. "And to Edmund. Tell him you shall make him a trade: for every social function he bids you attend, he must take you to a museum or lecture in return."

Juliet's eyes lit up, for this was the true attraction of London for her. She went because she must, because if she was to marry a gentleman, she must be fitted for the part of *lady*, but she cared little for feathers and fuss and would gladly eschew them all for the opportunity to explore London's many cultural delights.

"Now, that is a fine idea, Maddy!" she exclaimed, brightening at the prospect. "I shall tell him so this evening. Where do you think we ought to begin?"

Chapter Three

"Come in, come in! Welcome to London!" Mrs Angelica Brierley's eyes narrowed as she fixed them on Mr Turner. "Everyone except for *you*, brother. It has taken far too long for you to bring your delightful family up to town for a visit, and now I see you have brought only half of it!" She feigned disappointment, her heavy features arranged in a pout that she was able to hold for only a moment before dissolving into raucous laughter. "It is a very good job you brought the half that is my favourite!" Laying a conspiratorial arm around Louisa on one side and Juliet on the other, she ushered her two nieces towards a wide settee.

"You must not tell your sisters I said so, of course," she confessed, tweaking Louisa's blonde curls with a sigh. "Your hair! I envy you your golden curls, my dearest Lou -"

Louisa stiffened slightly. She had not been *Lou* in well over a year, although it would surely be the height of rudeness to remind her ageing aunt as much. She was saved from saying anything, though, as Mrs Brierley turned abruptly towards Juliet, forsaking Louisa to clasp her elder niece's hands in both of hers

"And I wish to hear all about the wedding plans and your handsome beau!" She giggled, as if the presence of young ladies made her young again herself. "Tell me, do your parents care for him?"

"We do," Mr Turner said, greeting his brother-in-law with a warm handshake and settling into a seat close to him. Mrs Turner hung back a little, clearly uncertain to which of the two parties she ought to show partiality, and hovering awkwardly between them until Mrs Brierley intervened.

"Oh, how dull! Sit down, dear, and tell me why you cannot bring yourself to disapprove of him just a little." She turned back to Juliet and continued speaking before Mrs Turner was able to summon a single word of response. "I do think love needs at least a little opposition to thrive. Too much acceptance leads to a very dreary life. Is he -" She paused, her lips pursing as if she could not quite bring herself to form the word. "Is he dreadfully *good*, then? There was never any hope for Bess or Maddy making anything other than respectable matches, and I dare say their young gentlemen are perfectly pleasant but dear me! Juliet, I held out rather higher hopes for you. Could you not find yourself an emigre count, a reformed scoundrel, somebody at least a little interesting?"

"I think Edmund is very interesting," Juliet said, rising in defence of *her boy*, for if anyone was to criticise him it should be her, and she would go to the ends of the earth to defend him against another.

"Edmund is interesting in theory," Louisa piped up, already tired of being overlooked in favour of Juliet, who, as the bride-to-be on this particular shopping trip, garnered most, if not all, attention. She sniffed, waiting a moment until she could be sure of attracting her aunt's attention entirely. "It is just that we have known him so long! I feel quite sure we know everything there is to know of him!"

"Well, that is no good!"

Juliet sucked in a sharp breath at this and was placated by a haphazard squeeze of her hand from her aunt, who continued to fix her inquisitive, watery eyes on Louisa as she spoke.

"It is always wise to reserve a little mystery surrounding one's husband until after you are married. Is that not right, my love?"

She lifted her voice to address the question to her husband, who harrumphed something that might have been agreement and continued his own whispered conversation with Mr Turner.

"I think it better one knows what one is letting oneself in for," Juliet protested. "For mystery, as you call it, might lead to disappointment -"

"Then again, it might not!" Aunt Brierley countered, with a wink that Louisa determined was solely directed at her. "Very well, I shall not cast aspersions on your young man, Juliet, at least not until I have met him. I trust I will be afforded the chance to meet him, while you are here? My brother did allude to the fact that he would be in London at this time too. I think it entirely above board if he dines with us here, so I might decide whether I think him worthy of my cleverest niece's affections."

Louisa sniffed, wondering what adjective was left to her, if Juliet was the *cleverest*.

"And as for you, Louisa," Aunt Brierley continued, with a knowing smile. "Don't fret, I shall not press you for details now, in such company as this, but do not think I shall forego quizzing you on your own romantic attachments...ah, yes! I spy a tiny hint of a blush on those apple cheeks of yours. I was quite persuaded that my *prettiest* niece should have at least half a dozen suitors. Tell me, please, there is at least one amongst *those* who we may consider at least a little mysterious."

Louisa pursed her lips, not quite able to keep her smile in check. Was Nash Weston mysterious? He was certainly charming, witty and fun in a way that Edmund could be, but with the added attraction of not having known Louisa all her life and sliding all too easily into the role of overbearing brother, which she did not care for. Nash never once strayed from the pigeon-hole of companion, and an admiring one at that. But could she consider him a suitor?

"My dear, do you plan to take tea, or is it your intention to deploy starvation as an interrogation technique?" Colonel Brierley asked, his tone dry and the merest hint of a sparkle in his grey eyes betraying his teasing.

"Tea!" Aunt Brierley clapped her hands. "Indeed, yes. Let us have tea. I have always found the sharing of secrets far more enjoyable in the presence of refreshments..."

"I HAVE MISSED THIS house!" Mrs Gale mused, stalking the corridors of the Gale's elegant London home ahead of her son.

"Well, it has been here all along and open to you, Mama, should you have chosen to visit."

His mother's continued iciness towards him tried Edmund's patience, and he seemed to notice it more now, in the absence of his friend, than less. He had thought, with Nash gone, it would afford mother and son some opportunity to talk, to have the argument that had been brewing ever since Mrs Gale first suspected Edmund's intent to propose to Juliet. She had first tried to sway him from his course by way of persuasion and when that had failed, had resorted to innumerable other minor forms of manipulation that would have worked rather better on the elder Mr Gale, had he still lived, than they ever had on her son.

Edmund had inherited his steely determination from his mother, along with his father's enviable good nature. But even the most even of temperaments could not bear such provocation forever.

"Oh, indeed! You would have me travel all this way unaccompanied, to wither here alone."

"Alone?" Edmund fingered his brow, pressing back against a headache that had been gradually encroaching al morning. Ordinarily, it might have been solved with a walk around one of London's many parks, or a trip to his club, wherein conversation with long-forgotten friends might offer some distraction. Leaving the house now, though, would mean leaving his mother and in her current mood that would be a further excuse to her to harden her grudge against him. Edmund screwed his eyes closed for one brief moment of oblivion before snapping his head up and meeting her gaze with a smile.

"You are not alone now, Mama, and I dare say you are right. We have neglected this house and our neighbours. What would you like to do first, now that we are here?" He swallowed. "I am entirely at my ease today, so please, do let us attend to whatever tasks and errands you wish to undertake."

His smile grew stretched almost to the point of pain. "I am at your service."

"Indeed." Mrs Gale's thin eyebrows arched, her tone icy. Edmund was poised to despair of ever winning over his Mama, of ever smoothing things between them, when she softened and retraced her steps, reaching up to smooth out the lines on his forehead with an almost affectionate touch.

"You oughtn't to frown, so. It ages you, and whilst some men become lines, you are not one of them." She dropped her hand to her side, smoothing some imagined dust from her skirts. "I suppose we might at least take a turn of the close. It is so long since I was last here that I scarcely recall our neighbours, and dare say they do not know me."

"Mama -" Edmund was poised to contradict her, to remind her that their neighbours were people very much like them, and whose townhouses were occupied in much the same manner. That was rarely, out of season. Still, this was the first hint Mrs Gale had shown that she might at least consider forgiving her son the capital sin of following his heart. He would not squander that. He dropped into a theatrical bow, unconsciously mimicking Nash as he straightened and beamed at her.

"I trust you will allow me to escort you, Mama. I should like to reacquaint myself with the close, too, for as you rightly assert it is quite some time since either of us were last here."

Mrs Gale harrumphed but said nothing, which minor point Edmund considered a victory.

The weather was not warm, despite the season, but it was at least dry. Their last week in the countryside had been punctuated by a run of rainy days, and Edmund could not deny that the presence of sunshine helped to lift his spirits. Even the chill of the breeze served to blow away the cobwebs of travel, and the last vestiges of his headache, so that both he and his mother were soon in better spirits than they had been for what felt like an age.

"I ought to call on Colonel and Mrs Brierley, I suppose," Edmund remarked aloud, as they reached a cross-roads and debated turning back towards home.

"Oh?" Mrs Gale's interest was piqued. Here was a name she did not recognise, and the fact that their home was the first beyond his own that Edmund should make mention of was a point of curiosity. Edmund almost smiled to think how quickly her interest would vanish when she learned of their true identity. A mischievous idea occurred to him, and he decided to delay true enlightenment, instead urging her to walk with him a little further along the bright, straight road, in a direction he had learned only one day previously, after a cursory examination of a map had brought to mind an address he had never yet had cause to visit.

"You shall like them, Mama. Good people. He was in the regiment -" Here, Mrs Gale's expression fell and Edmund sought to remind her of words she herself had uttered in favour of the military when in hearing of other ears than her son's. "I know how greatly you admire the regiment, Mama, and Colonel Brierley is as fine and upstanding a gentleman as ever I have known. Retired now, of course, but he is so amiable and engaging a fellow that he and his wife are quite the social pin on which a great portion of London society turns. You shall like them immensely."

"Brierley, you say?" Mrs Gale queried, frowning as if turning the name over in her mind. "Do you know, Edmund, I think I do recall some mention of them, now. Are they, perhaps, acquainted with Lady Dalrymple?" Her voice dropped to a near whisper. "The Prince Regent?"

Edward's eyebrows lifted and he nodded, unable to speak a word for fear that he would laugh and so betray himself. He did not doubt Juliet's aunt and uncle were quite as respectable a pair as any he might name in London, but he did not suppose they were any closer to the circles the Prince Regent moved in than he was - a fact that meant little enough to him.

"They live humbly, of course," Edmund ventured at last, as the street they walked along grew a little winding, a little shabbier, with the houses cramped a little closer together. He forestalled his mother's query, dropping his voice to denote a confidence. "In London, in any case. Of course, they are far more often found in Bath, for you know London can get so crowded these days."

Mrs Gale nodded as if this were a complaint she was fond of making, when, in truth, the crowds of London were what she most often craved on the long, empty evenings at Northridge.

"Here we are!" Edmund brightened as he beheld the house, thinking he would have recognised it anywhere from Juliet's colourful, amusing descriptions of the happy times she had spent here. He had wanted to claim her extravagant aunt and longsuffering uncle for his own the very first time he had heard her speak of them, and now, he realised with a grin, they would be. He stood a little taller as he approached the door, knocking sharply and waiting to be admitted to the parlour. Mrs Gale hesitated a step on the threshold, shooting a glance at her son as if she was not quite sure she trusted him or believed the words he had fed her on their winding walk here. But here, she was and it was too late to turn back.

They were shown into a parlour that was not small but made to feel it by an abundance of furniture, with paintings hanging on every available wall. Edward's eyes widened, and he smiled, turning to greet the owners of the house with all politeness before his gaze rested on his true reason for calling at the house that afternoon.

"Good afternoon, Juliet! I see you are all well settled, then? Mama, allow me to introduce you to Juliet's aunt and uncle. And of course, you recall *these* neighbours rather well. I assure you, they are only too familiar with you!"

Chapter Four

Their first day in London had been declared a success, even though they had spent the whole day at home. Edmund's visit had been a high point, and Juliet hoped he knew how pleased she was to see him and how well-received he had been in the home of her aunt and uncle.

His mother had been welcomed just as warmly but had certainly failed to make anything close to the good impression he had made.

"Now, Juliet!" Mrs Brierley remarked, bustling closer to her. "It is just us girls together, you may speak quite freely. Your Edmund's mother...!" She raised her thin eyebrows skywards and shuddered. "Is she always so..."

"Quiet?" Juliet grasped for a word she could use that would not be considered rude. Amongst friends, or with Edmund, even, she might have been a little freer in her choice, but Juliet knew her aunt well enough to know that she was liable to repeat anything she heard from her niece, neither caring nor noticing who might overhear her.

"Quiet is the very least that she was!" Mrs Brierley retorted, shaking her head with a disappointed sigh. "Dear me, Juliet, you shall have your work cut out with her for a mother-in-law."

Juliet's smile grew brittle. This, she did not need reminding of. As much as she looked forward to beginning her new life with Edmund - and she did, she reminded herself, as a bubble of excitement fizzed in her chest - the one obstacle in the way of her fully embracing the happy future that lay before her was Mrs Gale.

Juliet had entertained a fleeting hope that here, in London, things might be different between them. Edmund's mother might be able to see past the grudge she nursed against Juliet for having the audacity to win her son's heart and build some sort of understanding between them. She did not go so far as to ever think they might be friends, but if she could at least get past the wall of ice Mrs Gale had thrown up between them, she would count that a success.

"Still, I suppose we cannot help our mothers." Mrs Brierley sniffed, before dissolving into a smile that rendered her two decades younger. "Your Edmund is quite agreeable. And so clever! I had begun to abandon all hope of a gentleman managing to be both clever and handsome, and also good-humoured, and Mr Gale manages to be all three. I certainly approve of your choice, dear, and give you my leave to marry him."

This was enough to chase away any last vestiges of melancholy Juliet might still feel about the frosty reception she had received from Edmund's mother. Tucking her arm through her aunt's, she laughed, and the two ladies continued on their walk, pausing before various windows to examine the shopkeepers' wares and discuss the purchases that were ostensibly Juliet's reason for being in London.

"What a shame *your* Mama could not accompany us. And Louisa!" Mrs Brierley tutted. "I am surprised at Louisa. She is an artist. We would do well with her sense of taste and style."

Juliet frowned before realising that her aunt had not meant to snub her, and in any case, it was true: she was no great arbiter of style. If she wished to look the part of Mr Edmund Gale's wife, she could certainly do worse than take the advice of her stylish younger sister.

"Mama often suffers from headaches, especially after a day of travel and upheaval," she said, smiling in sympathy as she recalled the croaked excuse her mother had offered that morning, crying off the day shopping and bidding Juliet go on without her, and come home with her head filled with ideas that they might discuss together over tea.

That Louisa should refuse the opportunity of a shopping excursion was a mystery indeed, but she had claimed, rather haughtily, that she *wished to remain at home*. Juliet had no humour to tease the truth from her sister and decided that Louisa might keep her secrets, grateful for the chance of a morning with her aunt, who was always a great source of fun and adventure.

"Well, I shan't mind it," Mrs Brierley said, nestling her substantial frame a little closer to her slim niece. "I wished to speak with you alone, anyway."

Juliet felt herself colour, fearing for yet another pointed observation of either Edmund or his Mama. To her surprise, Mrs Brierley fixed her sharp eyes on her and smiled.

"I wish to know the status of your literary debut. Do not tell me that you have abandoned it, for if marriage forces you to forego your dream of authorship I shall march right over to Mr Gale's townhouse and inform my soon-to-be nephew-in-law that he must cease and desist, immediately, and allow my genius niece all leave to continue."

This little speech was so surprising and so fervent in its utterance, that Juliet laughed again, pleased and proud to have such an ardent supporter.

"I am no further along the road to publication," she confided. "But I am still writing."

She patted her reticule, which always housed a scrap of paper and writing implements, in case inspiration should strike when she was not at home.

"Good!" Mrs Brierley said, with a determined nod. "I do not like the thought of young ladies abandoning their own talents and enjoyments simply because they have had the fortune - good or bad - to marry. You must tell Bess as much, too. I care little that she is marrying a famed concert pianist if she abandons her path to becoming one in her own right."

"Aunt, you know Bes would never -" Juliet paused mid-thought, thinking that, before meeting Mr Cluett, she would not have thought it possible for Bess to form an attachment with any gentleman, let alone one whose name was known in the most elevated of circles. Perhaps Bess could become a famed musician, and Juliet did not doubt, with Mr Cluett by her side, that she might achieve it if she truly wished to. She sighed, fearing that her dreams remained just as far from her as they ever had been. Edmund might have promised never to keep her from writing, but that did not mean he would be able to help her pursue it.

"Now, look at this!" Mrs Brierley declared, tugging Juliet to a stop before a tall, elegant-looking building. She squinted at an announcement papered on one wall. "What providence! A lecture an authoress! Mrs Sinclair. And look, we have an hour to spare before it begins. Let us take tea and then return. Shopping can wait, don't you agree?"

Her eyes sparkled as she fixed them on her niece and Juliet was left certain that this had been her plan all along. Shopping might have been the excuse offered at home, but Juliet knew her aunt well enough to know that it was no accident that they should have found themselves faced with the announcement of a lecture by someone Juliet so longed to emulate. She opened her mouth to say so, but Mrs Brierley had already hurried off in the direction of the tearoom, leaving Juliet with little alternative than to hurry after her, smiling at the delightful turn their afternoon had taken.

NASH FUMBLED WITH HIS cuff, ensuring his aunt and cousin were comfortably seated before selecting his own chair beside his aunt. He glanced wearily towards the door, wishing he could escape through it, but there was no chance of his leaving, as a wall of guests arrived in pairs and small groups, and, in any case, his aunt had begun speaking again.

"...I do not approve of ladies writing *per se*," Mrs Reed continued, returning to the topic of the complaint that had been uppermost in her mind and most often on her lips that morning. "It is hardly a respectable accomplishment..."

She exchanged a knowing glance with Nash's cousin, who nodded, and waited for Nash to chime in with his approval. He made a sound that might have been an agreement, and Aunt Reed continued.

"And, of course, I much prefer to read things that are improving to one's mind and character. But they are very popular, these novels, and I had it on authority that a great number of people would be in attendance this afternoon - oh, Lady Bartlett! Good afternoon! Yes, do come and sit with us. Do you know Miss Abigail Carter? And this is my nephew, Mr Weston..."

Nash glanced up, his attention pulled once more to the endless round of introductions that seemed to follow him wherever he chanced to be with his aunt.

He had seen none of his friends since his return to London, more by his chance than by his choosing. He did not think even Aunt Reed was controlling enough to begrudge him an hour or two at the club, provided he caused no scandal. He smiled, drily, thinking that there was very little in his circle that she would not brand *scandal*, but he was determined to placate her and earn himself another few months' freedom at the end of this visit, so he went above and beyond mere obedience. He was her bondservant for the duration of his time in London, offering nought but agreeable conversation and a great many smiles and compliments, both to her and to his cousin.

He sighed, his gaze reaching across the bulk of his aunt to the slight, elbowy figure of Miss Abigail Carter. They scarcely knew one another, for all that they were related. *Cousin* denoted a closeness that was not there, for there were several removals in between, yet Aunt Reed had decided that theirs would be a perfect union, and he was running out of reasons to delay.

Would it be so dreadful? he asked himself, returning to the question that had kept him awake late into the night. Not every gentleman had the privilege of marrying for love, and he did not suppose Abigail would make him a terrible wife. She was not disagreeable nor ugly. She was not very much of anything, and therein lay the difficulty. Nash Weston was clever. He was fond of beauty and elegance and charm, eager for adventure and amusement. Could he endure a lifetime of…nothingness, merely to please his aunt?

And what is my alternative? He scowled, hurrying to smooth out the expression before it could be noticed, and lifting his gaze to his aunt and her companion. Both ladies were deep in a whispered discussion, their eyes darting across the room to their victim, an over-dressed woman who spoke loudly and theatrically to her own younger companion. Nash froze, recognising the young lady in an instance and stiffening, glancing around to see if he could spy her sister. But, no. Juliet Turner was there alone. *Small mercies.* Nash sank in his seat, hopeful that he could avoid being noticed.

The similarity of their positions at that moment was not lost on him, and he could not resist sneaking one last glimpse. Juliet's aunt, for that was who the lady must be, might have caught the attention and derision of his relative and her companions, but Nash could not help but be intrigued by her. She spoke eloquently and enthusiastically, winning several smiles from Juliet. He knew enough of Edmund's bride-to-be to know that to win her admiration was no mean feat, and he felt a fleeting wish that he might be playing escort to that pair of ladies instead of his own.

"…Mr Weston?"

He blanched, realising too late that he had allowed his attention to wander and had doubtless been noticed. He smiled, deploying all the charm his handsome features allowed and was pleased to see his interrogator colour and soften towards him immediately.

"Lady Bartlett." He kept his smile in place, knowing enough of psychology to gamble that in so doing he would encourage her to repeat her question without his ever having to admit he had not heard it.

"Yes, well, I merely wondered how you are enjoying London. It is some months since you were last here, I believe..."

"I was staying with a friend of mine in the country," Nash said, his smile slipping a little on the word *friend*. It was what Gale was, and he oughtn't to allow jealousy to undermine that. The fellow could hardly help it if fortune smiled on him. *And has been doing so since the day of his fortuitous birth!* Nash thought, bitterly.

"Mr Edmund Gale," Aunt Reed offered, evidently eager enough to trade on the association with one of London's eligible, wealthy bachelors.

"He is to be married, I believe!" Lady Bartlett declared, darting a glance almost unconsciously towards Nash.

"I am quite sure all young gentlemen are eager to be married after they have had their fill of freedom," Aunt Reed remarked, clearing her throat.

"Indeed!" Lady Bartlett beamed. "You shall have your own happy news to share before long, I don't doubt."

Aunt Reed smiled significantly but said nothing, settling into her chair and allowing her friend to do the same. Nash sighed. It would only be a matter of hours before news of his engagement was circulated amongst his aunt's set, and he had not even been permitted the opportunity to propose!

I wonder, he thought glumly. *If I may simply stand still and allow the whole of the wedding to happen around me...*

One knee jogged a little as he sat, a physical sign of his inward disquiet. He did not settle, despite the placid expression that remained pinned in place on his handsome features, and scarcely heard a word uttered by the famed novelist who came to address the crowd. His thoughts were elsewhere, stretching uselessly on to a future filled with comfort and wealth, an elegant home and the inheritance his aunt perpetually dangled over his head safely his to spend as he wished...

Marrying as his aunt chose was a small enough sacrifice to obtain all this, wasn't it? Why, then, did his eyes stray once more to the corner of the room dominated by Juliet Turner and her aunt? Why did his thoughts tease him with memories of the laughing, boisterous Turner parlour, of the sisters crowding around him, of one sister in particular, whose golden curls perpetually shone in the sunlight, bouncing as she spoke and laughed and danced...?

Chapter Five

Louisa had argued against joining Juliet and her aunt on their afternoon shopping expedition. It was not because she disliked shopping - quite the opposite! But she had woken in ill-humour and was tired of talk of weddings even before the family had finished their breakfast, so when the question was posed as to whether she would care to join their bridal reconnaissance, she had declined, claiming a preference to stay at home and rest.

Mama's excuse of a headache had been genuine, and Louisa had hovered outside her room for a quarter-hour to see whether she might be of some assistance. Selfish, she might be, but Louisa's compassion for her family was enough to overrule her comfort, particularly if they were unwell or otherwise unhappy. Mama was quite content to sleep, though, and bade her daughter *amuse herself and enjoy the day*, leaving Louisa with little in the way of entertainment. She was perusing her aunt and uncle's small library when her father knocked and entered, clad in his outerwear and with an expectant smile upon his face.

"My dear daughter!" he boomed. "I understand the thought of spending the afternoon shopping was considered rightly disagreeable to you..." His eyes twinkled with merriment as if he could well understand such a feeling, although he rather doubted its existence in his frivolous, spendthrift daughter. "I do hope you will not deny your old Papa the promise of your company. I wish to take a walk, and I wish that you might accompany me!" He offered her his arm in an old-fashioned show of chivalry and Louisa giggled, unable to refuse him and thinking, just then, that she actually might quite like to escape the house for an hour or so, especially if she might dictate their choice of location for walking.

"May we go to Regents' Park, Papa? I should like to see it in summer, when all the flowers are blooming and full of life!"

This was only a partial untruth. She was fond of beauty in all its guises and knew by reputation the elegance of the display in all of London's parks would far outstrip anything she might have seen at home. But Louisa's preference for Regents' Park had more to do with the potential for people-watching the park promised.

"I think we can manage that," Mr Turner said, his eyes twinkling at her as if he saw through her ruse immediately but would never say as much. He indulged each of his daughters in their own way, but it was no secret that Louisa, as the baby of the family, received the most spoiling from both of her parents.

They followed a meandering path towards the park, pausing every so often so Mr Turner could re-orient himself with their location, or so that he could make some or other observation of the historic significance of a place. Louisa bore this with all patience, but her interest in history could not begin to rival Juliet's, so the digressions were fleeting at best until, at last, they reached the park.

"Well!" Mr Turner declared, as they found their pace and began to walk. "I did not expect to see so many people here! It seems half of London has had the same idea as us."

"Indeed!" Louisa agreed, happily allowing her eyes to roam over the crowds. She hungrily took in all the details of style and colour favoured by the ladies she passed, for it seemed to her than even the least extravagantly dressed were far more fashionable than anybody she might see at home. She reached a hand up to her hair, tugging thoughtfully on her curls as she examined an exquisite bonnet atop a cascade of dark hair and wondered if she might manage to modify the style and make it her own.

"How strange it is to walk past all these people and not see a soul one knows!" Mr Turner remarked after he and Louisa had walked some way in silence, greeting strangers as they passed with nods and waves of acknowledgement.

"I rather like it!" Louisa said, lifting her chin and beaming as she noticed a young gentleman so taken with her that he narrowly avoided colliding with a tree. He recovered himself and hurried on, blushing and burying his head in his hand.

"Ah, here is *one* person we know!" Mr Turner's voice boomed joyously and he lifted his hand in a wave. "And someone even you may prefer to a sea of fashionable strangers, my dear!" He lowered his voice, nudging Louisa gently with his elbow and nodding to a trio of people some way ahead of them. "Tell me, is that not our old friend Mr Weston?"

The words were barely uttered when Louisa's eyes fixed on the familiar figure of Edmund's friend and it took all her powers to resist the urge to run up and greet him. But, no. She was in London now, and she must act as these fashionable strangers might. She must show Nash that she was not *little Louisa*, a young companion he might tease and admire by turns, but someone old enough to know her own mind, to love and be loved.

"Well?" Mr Turner urged. "I am surprised at you, Lou. I thought you would be the first to suggest we ought to bowl up and say hello."

"We may greet him," Louisa said, trialling a new, imperious tone of voice that surely distinguished her as elegant and aloof. It was certainly different, for her father frowned to hear it, and she cleared her throat and tried again, sounding a little more like her usual self. "Look, we are about to pass them. It would be rude of us *not* to acknowledge the acquaintance."

"Quite so," Mr Turner said, his lips quirking as he looked away from his daughter to the oncoming trio. He dipped his head, touching his hat in a show of recognition. "Good day, Mr Weston!"

Louisa had dropped her head, peering up at Nash through her eyelashes in the most beguiling way she could manufacture, so she could not be sure at first what his response was. He said nothing, though, and as she lifted her head, she saw his gaze sweep over them, with nought but the very vaguest of smiles. There was the slightest wave, a tiny nod of the head, and then he was gone, ushering his two companions - one older lady and one young, Louisa noticed, with a lurch - further along the path.

Mr Turner said nothing, and when Louisa looked at him, his expression was one of disappointment. He recovered himself almost immediately with a smile and patted Louisa's hand in silent encouragement.

"I dare say he did not see us, my dear. Or perhaps he was running late for a pressing engagement. No matter. I have no doubt our paths will cross again in time."

"WHO WAS THAT?"

The question had come from Abigail's thin lips, her voice as pale and thin as its owner, and Nash was so unused to hearing her speak at all that he almost missed it this time, and did not respond until his aunt, with rather less subtlety of manner, repeated the question.

"Yes, Nash, who were those people?"

Nash resisted the urge to look back, to *walk* back and greet his friends properly. For they were his friends. Louisa was...*Louisa*. Yet how could he say that to his aunt, to Abigail?

"Friends..." he mumbled, then, realising he had spoken aloud, he clarified. "Friends of Edmund's. You recall, Aunt, Edmund Gale, who I visited this past Spring."

"Ah, yes." His aunt's eyes narrowed. "They certainly seemed to remember you."

"I am rather memorable," Nash said, with a sly grin that ordinarily won his aunt over to his side. It was just as successful this time, for she held his gaze for half a moment before dissolving in giggles.

"Yes, my dear nephew, indeed you are! Now, would you escort me over to that bench, I am a little weary of walking and wish to rest a moment. Abigail, dear, you are surely in need of some rest, too."

Abigail dear looked momentarily mutinous, but her neutral expression was in place before Nash could be sure it had ever slipped. *A pity*, he thought, as his aunt leaned rather heavily on his arm and he steered her towards a seat. *I might have been a little intrigued by an Abigail with the ability to think for herself!*

His womenfolk comfortably situated, Nash straightened, standing by to receive his next orders and certain they would be given before long. His aunt was content at that moment to merely sit, though, and to reflect on their afternoon's entertainment.

"She was amusing enough, I suppose..." Mrs Reed spoke of the authoress whose talk had been engaging enough that even Nash had found his attention captivated. "And quite pretty! I was surprised. But not married." There was such dismissal in his aunt's tone that Nash felt his own lips curve upwards in a smile. As if marriage was a woman's only goal and purpose.

"She did not seem to mind it, though," Abigail ventured.

Nash was surprised to hear this, and glanced at his cousin, fancying he saw a glimmer of rebellion in her watery blue eyes. "Perhaps her books gave her the fulfilment she needed."

"Yes, and the income." His aunt harrumphed. "She was only able to pursue publishing on account of her wealthy brother. Without him to bankroll her silly little stories, I do not suppose she would have such vaunted success or such enthusiasm for the task."

"I have read one or two of her books," Abigail continued, and Nash did his best to disguise his surprise, particularly at his cousin's last words. "I rather enjoyed them."

"Enjoyed -? Ah, well, you are young." Mrs Reed reached out and patted her hand, stiffly. "I shall not begrudge you a little entertainment, and we do all have our foibles. Take Mr

Weston, here, standing so nobly to attention and with all care towards our wellbeing. He wasted far too many hours in his youth running about London with his gadabout friends, misbehaving." Her eyes sparkled to suggest she was teasing him, but there was a hardness in his voice that did not entirely lend itself to humour. "Many a time was I asked to bail him out of one scrape or another." Mrs Reed laughed a loud, barking laugh, shaking her head to dismiss the observation. "We must indulge you youngsters in your youthful indiscretions." She sighed. "Of course, none of them did you too great a harm, and now see what a charming pair you make!"

Nash glanced at Abigail, then, surprised to see a flicker of dislike in the features she turned towards him. Again, the expression was gone almost before he could remark upon it, a serene sort-of smile in its place.

His aunt cleared her throat, as if urging him to follow her comments with a word or two of his own, and he struggled to summon anything, at first. He turned towards the horizon again, his eyes tracing back along the path which had lately taken them past Mr Turner and Louisa, and regretting he was not a braver person. He ought to have acknowledged them at least, if not stopped to share a word or two. He might have introduced them to his aunt and his cousin...but, no. That was foolishness. If he could pretend to himself to care nothing for Louisa's pretty smiles and easy temperament, his aunt would see through the charade in an instant. She would compare the way he acted around Louisa to the way he acted around his cousin and recognise the truth, and all would be lost.

"I am grateful you bear with me as graciously as you do, aunt," he said, woodenly, knowing that this was not quite the compliment his aunt was fishing for, but also certain that it would placate her.

"Gratitude?" Mrs Reed giggled, but the sound grated on Nash's nerves all the worse for his knowledge that it was faked. "I do not need your gratitude, Nash. You are my nephew. I want only what is best for you. Come, dear. Are you rested? Let us walk on a little further before returning home. It always serves one well to see and be seen in Regents' Park. One never knows quite whose path one might cross...!"

Without being asked, Nash bent and helped first his aunt and then his cousin to their feet. He was a little slow in releasing his grip on Abigail and found that she did not immediately move away from him, but seemed scarcely to notice he was there at all.

"Nash!" Mrs Reed barked, reaching out for him, and he forsook Abigail for his aunt with an apologetic smile that barely seemed to register with her. His aunt's grip was tighter, her hold on him heavier, so that there was no chance at all of his escaping. How much her hold on his life felt like that at present! He might have wished to greet Louisa Turner as the friend she had been to him in, he might wish she could be a friend to him again now, or more, even! But there was no hope for it, not while his aunt so firmly directed his steps.

If only I had a fortune of my own! he thought, his eyes fixed on the ground before him. *If only I might not need her - I might live just as I chose, and I should not choose* this. He allowed his thoughts to stray, easily and happily to another whose arm might rest gently in his, whose steps would match his, pace for pace, and whose biting observations would amuse, rather than irritate him. How different his life might be, if only...!

Chapter Six

Edmund and Mrs Gale smiled and bade their hosts farewell, before embarking on the short walk to the next house they would be calling at.

"I trust you will not object to our staying longer than the specified quarter-hour at *this* house?"

Mrs Gale's voice was polite, but Edmund knew her well enough not to miss the thinly-veiled criticism she levied at him. Ordinarily, he might fight back, but this time he merely bowed his head and smiled.

"We may stay just as long as you wish to, Mama. Assuming, of course, that our hosts are content to have us."

Mrs Gale scowled at him, before hurrying to settle her features into her usual sanguine smile. Edmund was not sure if she was annoyed with him for suggesting their hosts might not care to keep them all afternoon, or because he refused to let her bait him. Either way, he straightened, offering her his arm with all the politeness he could muster.

"I am grateful you allow me to occupy your time so completely today, Edmund," she declared, offering him an imperious little head-tilt. "I thought for certain that you would prefer to spend all day with your fiancée."

"Juliet is busy this afternoon, Mama. She is spending some time with her family. Besides..." He slowed, as they drew within sight of the Grenvilles' house. "I could hardly leave you to make your calls unaccompanied, could I?" He knocked smartly on the door, turning his attention to the servant who ushered them in, and ignoring his mother's evident annoyance with him. She would tire of her games sooner or later, he supposed, and at least if she was directing her anger, however stiffly, towards him, then Juliet was spared the brunt of it.

"Mrs Gale! Edmund! Good afternoon!"

He brightened at the warmth of the reception he received, recalling that he had always found the Grenvilles the most interesting of Mama's London friends.

"I hear there are wedding bells in your future, Edmund!" Mrs Grenville sparkled, looking easily a decade younger than her years. "Come, sit by me and tell me all about it."

"You might have brought the young lady with you, Edmund! You should know we would be happy to meet her."

Mr Grenville ushered Mrs Gale to a chair, but his attention remained on Edmund, much to Mrs Gale's evident annoyance.

"You will meet Juliet in time," Edward promised his hosts. "She is in London, so perhaps we might even contrive a meeting before we return to home."

"Wonderful!" Mr Grenville turned to Mrs Gale. "And you must be pleased to see your son so happily matched, Mrs Gale." He waggled his eyebrows at her. "It is all we parents can hope for, is not it?"

Mrs Gale sniffed but did not contradict him, and when her eyes met Edmund's there was some shadow there he had not noticed before. Before he could puzzle it out, though, Mrs Grenville had laid a light hand on his arm, drawing his attention back to her.

"She has sisters, I believe?"

"Three of them." Edmund smiled. "One has joined the family in London, where they stay with an aunt and uncle...Colonel and Mrs Brierley."

This was uttered despite his Mama choosing that precise moment to clear her throat, and Edmund was forced to conclude this was not coincidental but an attempt, by Mrs Gale, to avoid disclosing what close connections they now had with residents on the edge of Cheapside.

"I do not think I know the name," Mrs Grenville said, oblivious to the look that was exchanged between mother and son. She beamed at Edmund. "Perhaps you would be kind enough to introduce us, during your time in London."

"You shall attend Thursday's assembly, of course." This was a statement of fact, although Mr Grenville did at least look to Mrs Gale for confirmation. "A visit to London is not complete without at least one assembly, or so my wife assures me."

"Quite so!" Edmund agreed, with a grin. He liked assemblies and was pleased by the Grenvilles eagerness to meet Juliet and support their union. It was a reception so unlike that which he had received, and continued to receive, from his Mama that he was poised to invite them to the wedding, if only so he might be guaranteed as warm a reception from his side of the church as he might have from Juliet's. He turned to his mother, sensing that this would be an opportune moment to gain her agreement, for she was duty-bound, before friends, to be agreeable.

"You have spoken of little other than the assembly since our trip to town was first mooted, haven't you, Mama? I know you are so fond of a chance to dance and be amongst friends."

sight of the Grenvilles' house. "I could hardly leave you to make your calls unaccompanied, could I?" He knocked smartly on the door, turning his attention to the servant who ushered them in, and ignoring his mother's evident annoyance with him. She would tire of her games sooner or later, he supposed, and at least if she was directing her anger, however stiffly, towards him, then Juliet was spared the brunt of it.

"Mrs Gale! Edmund! Good afternoon!"

He brightened at the warmth of the reception he received, recalling that he had always found the Grenvilles the most interesting of Mama's London friends.

"I hear there are wedding bells in your future, Edmund!" Mrs Grenville sparkled, looking easily a decade younger than her years. "Come, sit by me and tell me all about it."

"You might have brought the young lady with you, Edmund! You should know we would be happy to meet her."

Mr Grenville ushered Mrs Gale to a chair, but his attention remained on Edmund, much to Mrs Gale's evident annoyance.

"You will meet Juliet in time," Edward promised his hosts. "She is in London, so perhaps we might even contrive a meeting before we return to home."

"Wonderful!" Mr Grenville turned to Mrs Gale. "And you must be pleased to see your son so happily matched, Mrs Gale." He waggled his eyebrows at her. "It is all we parents can hope for, is not it?"

Mrs Gale sniffed but did not contradict him, and when her eyes met Edmund's there was some shadow there he had not noticed before. Before he could puzzle it out, though, Mrs Grenville had laid a light hand on his arm, drawing his attention back to her.

"She has sisters, I believe?"

"Three of them." Edmund smiled. "One has joined the family in London, where they stay with an aunt and uncle...Colonel and Mrs Brierley."

This was uttered despite his Mama choosing that precise moment to clear her throat, and Edmund was forced to conclude this was not coincidental but an attempt, by Mrs Gale, to avoid disclosing what close connections they now had with residents on the edge of Cheapside.

"I do not think I know the name," Mrs Grenville said, oblivious to the look that was exchanged between mother and son. She beamed at Edmund. "Perhaps you would be kind enough to introduce us, during your time in London."

"You shall attend Thursday's assembly, of course." This was a statement of fact, although Mr Grenville did at least look to Mrs Gale for confirmation. "A visit to London is not complete without at least one assembly, or so my wife assures me."

"Quite so!" Edmund agreed, with a grin. He liked assemblies and was pleased by the Grenvilles eagerness to meet Juliet and support their union. It was a reception so unlike that which he had received, and continued to receive, from his Mama that he was poised to invite them to the wedding, if only so he might be guaranteed as warm a reception from his side of the church as he might have from Juliet's. He turned to his mother, sensing that this would be an opportune moment to gain her agreement, for she was duty-bound, before friends, to be agreeable.

"You have spoken of little other than the assembly since our trip to town was first mooted, haven't you, Mama? I know you are so fond of a chance to dance and be amongst friends."

"Amongst *friends*, yes," Mrs Gale equivocated. "The public assemblies, on the other hand…"

"Oh, I know they can be a little overcrowded," Mr Grenville agreed, his booming voice quickly overshadowing Mrs Gale's dainty protests. "And one is pressed into society with a great swathe of people one might not ordinarily see or speak to, but…" He beamed, his enthusiasm rendering him almost youthful. "It is such jolly good fun, is it not, my dear?"

Mrs Grenville said nothing, but nodded, smiling indulgently.

"I think we shall be forced to attend, Mama, do not you think so?" Edmund could not resist pressing his mother to a confirmation, here, surrounded by those she would not countenance disappointing. He had always enjoyed assemblies, be they large or small, and he would enjoy this one all the more with Juliet on his arm. "I know you have so often been disappointed by the simple public assemblies we are forced to join at home. Let us go and see how easily London outshines them!"

There was a moment of brittle silence when Edmund was sure he could see the gears of his mother's mind working furiously to fabricate some kind of excuse, anything that might permit her to punish her son for his impudence, whilst not disappointing her friends, but she could summon nothing. The loud chime of a grandfather clock broke the spell, and she fixed a furious glare on her son.

"Dear me! Is that a quarter-hour gone already? You must forgive us for only a fleeting visit today, Mrs Grenville, Mr Grenville. You know what sons are like, and mine has been intimating all day that he would rather be elsewhere."

Edmund's smile tightened, seeing the game she was playing and finding no immediate way to manoeuvre free. His hosts were most genial, though, and, whilst disappointed to lose their guests so soon, did not seem unduly offended by their swift departure.

"Until the assembly!" Mr Grenville called, waving them off. "We shall look forward to seeing you there!"

"AND TO THINK, SHE ACCOMPLISHED all of those things whilst being a wife and a mother!" Juliet fairly floated home after enjoying the lecture with her aunt. She had been able to meet and share a word or two of conversation with Mrs Sinclair, courtesy her aunt's bravely marching up to introduce them at the moment that Juliet's courage had failed. Not only that, but several other ladies there had been of especial interest to her. Not one of them would have pleased her mother or sister, for all of them were dressed somewhat shabbily or unfashionably, but Juliet had come home with her imagination enlivened, and her hands itched to write.

"Ah, Juliet! Here you are. Good afternoon, Sister, did you enjoy your shopping time?"

"Shopping?" Juliet kissed her father on the cheek but dismissed his question with a derisive snort. "Shopping was the very least of our occupation this afternoon. We went to a lecture by a real, live authoress!"

"Yes," Mrs Reed confessed, greeting her brother with an apologetic smile. Shopping was, I confess, merely an excuse to spirit Juliet out of doors and use her for my own nefarious ends. I was afraid, if I confessed my wish to take her to see Mrs Sinclair, you would have prevented the expedition."

"Prevented it?" Mr Turner laughed. "Whatever for? She is no purveyor of scandal, is she, this Mrs Sinclair?" He frowned. "I confess I have not read any of her books, but I have heard them remarked upon..."

"She was wonderful!" Juliet sighed, sinking theatrically into a settee and realising, belatedly, that she had almost smothered her sister. "Oh, Louisa! Why are you sitting here in the way?"

"I wasn't *in* the way," Louisa countered, tremulously. "You might have looked before sitting on me!"

Juliet obediently shifted to the side, eyeing her sister with surprise. Louisa's normally perfect hair was a little unkempt, as if she had tugged her hand through it many times that afternoon, and her face looked splotchy from tears.

"Is something the matter?" she asked, reaching out to smooth down the worst of the disarray.

"Nothing!" Louisa squawked, dodging out of her sister's grasp. She drew in a shaky breath. "I merely do not see the thrill of listening to an old woman drone on about writing all afternoon."

"That's because you were not there," Mrs Reed said, mildly, sitting in her chair and reaching for her fan. "She spoke eloquently and amusingly. What was that anecdote she shared with us about her friend, the Countess of Marlborough?"

"Oh, even *you* shall laugh at this one, Lou," Juliet began, clearing her throat. Louisa shot her a look, and sniffed tremulously, causing Juliet to lose her enthusiasm for the story.

"Perhaps I shall wait and share it later when Mama can be with us and hear it too." She turned to her father. "Is she feeling any better?"

"A little," Mr Turner said, with a reassuring smile. "She plans to join us for dinner."

"I should hope so!" Mrs Reed remarked, scarcely concealing her disdain for her sister-in-law's weak constitution. "I have never known such a one for headaches and poor health as you wife..." She was silenced by a warning look from her husband, and said no more, focusing her attention on her fan, for it was a warm day, and their walk home had not been a short one.

"Well, what have you been about today, Louisa?" Juliet asked, eager to brighten her sister's mood and knowing, from years of practice, that being allowed to speak about herself and her interests was sure to do it. This time, to her surprise, Luisa's blue eyes filled once more with tears, and she said nothing. It fell to Mr Turner to offer an answer, which he did, in his usual calming manner.

"We went for a walk. Your sister was kind enough to accompany me on my daily constitutional, and we took a turn about Regents' Park, which is as pretty as ever I have seen it, although rather crowded with walkers!"

Mrs Reed sniffed, launching into a long explanation of why her poor, countrified brother ought to have chosen to visit one of the other parks if he wished to walk without battling crowds and Juliet turned once more to look at her sister. Louisa's face was downcast, and Juliet reached out to take her hand, squeezing it gently, a silent question. Louisa did not look up at her but wriggled her hand free.

"I think I shall go and check on Mama," she announced, her voice trembling as if she fought off still more unshed tears.

"Let me come with you," Juliet offered, eager to get to the bottom of whatever had so upset her sister. Louisa let out a long sigh but did not stop her, and together the two girls slipped out of the parlour, pulling the door closed just as Mrs Reed called after them.

"Do see if she would care to join us for some refreshments, won't you? I am sure your Mama is quite well enough to walk downstairs and take tea with us..."

"I am sorry you did not join us today," Juliet began, trying in vain to know how best to encourage intimacy with her prickliest of sisters. If this were Bess, she should have no problem in managing her. But of her three sisters, Juliet's relationship with Louisa had always been fraught with difficulty. She drew a breath. "We did pass some very elegant looking places, and I shall need your eye for style if I am to purchase anything at all." She smiled. "I know how you like to give out advice, and you have always been better than me at appreciating beauty."

Louisa sniffed but said nothing.

"I imagine the flowers in the park were quite lovely at this time of year. You must tell me which beds you liked best, so I can look out for them."

Still nothing and Juliet began to feel a little annoyed. She was trying her best to be a good sister, and offer Louisa a listening ear. If she did not wish to confide in her, then perhaps it was not worth trying further. *I do not suppose there is anything so very wrong! Louisa has always made a drama out of every little thing.*

She abandoned the attempt, and it was in silence the two young ladies climbed the last few steps and knocked lightly on the door of Mrs Turner's room.

"Come in!" Their mother's voice was bright but betrayed her tiredness, and Juliet immediately shifted the focus of her concern from her sister to Mrs Turner, who was sitting up in bed, a light blanket pulled over her laps, as she worked on some embroidery.

"Mama! You are looking better than you did this morning. Pray, come downstairs and join us for tea, won't you?"

"That is a very nice idea!" Mrs Turner declared, laying down her sewing and reaching up to tuck a stray curl or two safely in place. "I have been antisocial far too long today. Tell me, dear, how did your shopping trip with Aunt Reed go?" Her tone was neutral, her affection for her daughter and eagerness to hear about the day far outstripping any awkwardness of feeling that might still exist between Mrs Turner and her sister-in-law, even after so many years.

"We did not go shopping at all!" Juliet confided, swallowing a laugh as she told of her day's adventures. "It was all a ruse! Do not you think it cunning of Aunt to do so, to ensure that we were able to attend Mrs Sinclair's lecture?"

Mrs Turner frowned, her smile dimming a little.

"You do not mind me having seen her, do you? It was a public lecture, and a great many women were there -" Juliet feared, for a moment, that her mother did not approve of the event, and wondered why, when Mrs Turner had never made any show of disapproving of her writing, she should not wish for her to see a real, live authoress speak in person.

"Of course I do not mind it," Mrs Turner said, her smile lifting. "But I do not see why Aunt Reed felt the need to lie about your plans for the day. Anyway, I am sure she had her reasons. Come, girls, let us go downstairs, for the promise of tea has quite revived me!"

She slid an arm around both of her daughters, and Juliet could not help but notice the way Louisa stiffened at their mother's touch, moving away from her as they passed through the doorway.

Chapter Seven

Louisa tilted her cup this way and that, watching the way the light rippled across the surface of the rapidly-cooling tea she hadn't drunk and trying to look as if she was interested in what Juliet was saying. She and her aunt had been talking for what felt like an hour, telling and retelling all about the lecture they had been to, what Mrs Sinclair had looked like, sounded like, talked about...

Stifling a yawn, Louisa lifted the cup to her lips and took the tiniest sip, grimacing as she realised just how cold her tea had become, and placing the cup and saucer down on the table beside her, folding her hands in her lap and praying her posture didn't betray her boredom.

"You are very quiet, Luisa!" Aunt Brierley observed, her eyes narrowing as she fixed her gaze on her youngest niece. "Quite a change from the usual, I am sure!" She let out a theatrical sigh. "Please don't tell me you are becoming decorous and agreeable in your old age. I do so disapprove of young ladies losing their spark, and you, my dear, had plenty!"

Louisa smiled, pleased to be noticed and complimented in such a way, and even more pleased because their aunt had spoken across Juliet to do so. She was tired of conversing about the lady-author and wished for a change, too.

"I am quite well, Auntie," Louisa said, tilting her head and appreciating the bounce of her blonde curls which she knew was becoming.

"We enjoyed our walk in the park, did not we, Louisa?" Mr Turner said, leaning patting her arm, gently. "I dare say my energetic young daughter would have happily remained out of doors even longer, had I not grown weary and longed for the comforts of home."

Louisa's smile froze, as she recalled the very reason she and her father had hastily returned home. It had not been weariness, either his or hers, but a silent agreement that their jaunt had been rather spoiled by the utter lack of acknowledgement they had received from their friend Mr Weston.

"Indeed, it seems poor Louisa is disappointed by the mere memory of being forced to return home before her time!" Aunt Brierley was watching, shrewdly, and drawing her own conclusions from the way her niece's features fell into a pout. "Was there some reason you were so eager to remain in Regents Park, my dear?" Her eyes sparkled with fun. "Perhaps some *person*....?"

Louisa flinched, wondering just how apparent her feelings must have been for her aunt to draw such an accurate conclusion.

"Yes! I think that must be it. All the young folk favour Regents' Park!" Mrs Brierley clapped her hands. "Tell me, do, who was the handsome stranger who caught your eye? I dare say he was handsome?"

"There was no stranger, Auntie," Louisa managed, dropping her gaze to her knees.

"No, but we did pass a friend," Mr Turner mused, nursing his chin in his hand. "At least, I thought we did - you recall, dear," he turned to his wife, his features pinched in a vague smile. "Mr Weston." He turned to include his sister in the conversation. "A friend of our neighbour - of Edmund's. He spent the best part of the spring at Northridge and I am not sure an afternoon went by when he did not find some cause to call at our parlour." His smile fell. "It seems his friendliness does not extend to passing us in the park, though, for, alas, he did not seem to recognise us, did he, Louisa?"

"Not recognise you?"

It was Juliet who spoke, her own eyes narrowed in suspicion. She fixed her gaze on Louisa, who sank further into her seat and prayed her expression did not betray her.

"He was busy, I think, Papa," Louisa managed, her voice low. "He had company, after all."

"I wonder -" Mrs Turner began, but before she could say another word, the butler arrived at the door to the parlour, announcing with a flourish the arrival of a guest.

"Mr Gale."

Louisa let out a breath of relief, pleased that Edmund had arrived and would now distract her aunt, freeing her from scrutiny.

"Mrs Brierley! And Turners, all." His face crinkled in a smile and he dropped in a droll little bow, before rising again and holding his hand up in triumph. "I have a proposition!"

"Oh?" Mrs Brierley chuckled at this effusive show of chivalry and patted the seat next to her. "Come and sit down, you energetic young man, and tell us what has you so excited!"

"An assembly, my dear Aunt." He winked at the possessive use of this title, which he had no true claim to and would not have until after he and Juliet were married. It made her blush and giggle, though, and Louisa smiled to see her ageing aunt so unsettled by Edmund's trademark familiarity and cheer.

"An assembly?" It was Juliet who questioned him, glancing over at Louisa surprised that it was not she who declared so excitedly of the promised entertainment.

"Indeed! And we are all to attend!" He fixed a triumphant smile on Louisa as he folded both his arms and his legs and surveyed the room, evidently delighted with himself and with this promised treat. "There, Miss Louisa. Do not complain that nothing exciting ever happens now! I have sent word to Nash to join us, too, so we shall have a jolly old time, all together!"

Louisa smiled, feeling hope flare in her chest. If there was to be an assembly, and Nash was invited, maybe it truly would be like old times.

Perhaps he did not mean to ignore us this afternoon, she thought. He surely would not do so at an assembly but would smile and laugh and dance with her precisely as he had done at home. *And if he does not...* She lifted her chin, feeling a flicker of her old imperiousness return to her. *There are bound to be a great deal of other elegant, charming young gentlemen who will. Who needs an engagement, when I shall have my pick of suitors?*

"AN ASSEMBLY! HOW DELIGHTFUL!" Mrs Reed exclaimed, with a sly look at Nash.

He sat in his aunt's grand parlour, turning over the note from Edmund, which had accompanied the notice of the assembly, and a none-too-subtle invitation that Nash *and his household* must join the festivities and stop hiding away from associations with old friends.

This last he had not read aloud, certain that his aunt would seize upon the comment and demand its explanation, and because he felt somewhat pricked by his conscience. Hiding away. That was precisely what he was doing, was it not? It was that which had made him shrink back in his seat at the lecture, and avoid being noticed by Juliet and her aunt. It was that that made him entirely ignore Louisa and her father when he passed them in the park, choosing to pretend he had not seen them rather than to stop and greet them as the friends they were. *Or had been,* he thought, sourly. They could be friends no longer, for his aunt would not abide it, nor could he even conceive of continuing a friendship with Louisa. He must abandon his past hopes and enjoyments and embrace his present and future, the very young lady who sat not three feet away from him, chatting animatedly over the promised evening of dancing and celebration.

"I do not make a habit of going to the public assemblies, you understand," his aunt was saying, punctuating each of her words with an embroidery stitch. "Their doors are open to any who should wish to attend, after all..."

Nash rolled his eyes, hiding his face behind his letter to obscure his disdain from the aunt who would be sure to take offence at such a reaction.

"It is different for you young folk, of course." She smiled indulgently at Abigail, but her smile died as she looked over at her nephew. "And I understand Nash made a great habit of attending them when he was last in town."

Nash winced. This was true, of course, for he had very much enjoyed attending every assembly, dinner and soiree he was invited to, finding it easy and enjoyable to make friends and be around jolly, pleasing people, regardless of their social standing. He had been making the most of his freedom, while it was afforded him, of course, but he could not say as much now, not while Abigail was within hearing.

"They offer a chance to see friends, Aunt, nothing more."

"A great deal more!" his aunt remonstrated. "Why, that is the danger! Many young ladies attend such evenings with the sole intent of securing for themselves a husband, and young men are none too aware of the danger they place themselves in. Oh, it is all well and good to dance and be merry, but who knows what strings are laid ready to entangle your nimble feet."

"I dance well enough to avoid them," Nash countered, dropping his voice to obscure his last word from hearing. "Usually."

"Do you know, Mr Weston, we have never before danced together!" Abigail exclaimed as if this were a scandalous predicament and one that must be remedied as soon as possible. "I hope you will not begrudge me the opportunity at this assembly, for I shall know no-one else, and be bound to be a wallflower if not."

"As if you could ever be a wallflower, my dear!" Aunt Reed remonstrated. "You are too pretty, too agreeable. No, your problem will not be a lack of interest, I dare say, but too much. You must not abandon poor Nash for his friends, for he is sure to feel a little possessive of his soon-to-be bride."

Nash stiffened at these words, although they were not unexpected. Although he had not formally offered his proposal to Abigail, it was clear that he could do little to delay the dreadful day. His aunt's hints had grown increasingly specific, and increasingly pointed, and he was quite certain that if he did not make a move towards marriage then she would announce the engagement herself, regardless, before too many more days passed. The die was cast, and Nash must act, one way or another.

He turned Edmund's note over in his hands, his eyes resting idly on his friend's rushed cursive. *No more hiding away from your old friends, for you are missed!* How *he* missed *them*. It had been a fine time, the months he had spent in the countryside. How many hours had he wasted in running over to call on the Turners, and how warm had been his welcome! He glanced over at Abigail, wondering how different this empty, icy parlour might feel if it was gregarious, charming Louisa sitting in her seat. She would win his aunt over, surely, by virtue of her beauty and grace. *If only she had a little money!* His aunt might make allowances for many things, but she would not see his inheritance fall into the hands of a fortune-hunter, and no matter how agreeable Louisa was, that was what his aunt would see her as.

Perhaps I could love her enough to give up the fortune I have been promised. This idea was a new one, one that he had not dared to entertain before now. Was it possible to be happy without a cushion of wealth upon which to sit? He might marry Louisa, but they would never be afforded the comforts he now enjoyed. Even she would be forced to abandon what little comfort she had, as the daughter of a country gentleman. She was too fond of beauty, of elegance, to ever entertain such a sacrifice. *It would be a disaster*, he counselled himself, his hand tightening around the note and crushing it into a ball. *We would end up resenting one another.* No, better she despise him now than grow to hate him over time. Better he learn to accept his fate and maintain his status.

"I am looking forward to meeting all your friends, Mr Weston, so you must take great care to introduce me!" Abigail cooed, looking over at him with a cloying expression of devotion that made Nash shudder. "After all, once we are married, they shall be my friends too!"

He thought of clever, quick-witted Edmund, of Juliet's sharp tongue, and realised with a sinking feeling that this was simply not true. They would tolerate Abigail on his behalf, but they would never be friends. Slowly, his old companions would slide from his grasp and he would be left with an elegant estate, but a wife he did not like.

Can such a trade possibly be worth making?

Chapter Eight

Juliet was used to being one of the first in her family to wake of a morning, but in London it seemed even more pronounced. She tiptoed downstairs, not wanting to disturb anyone. She and Louisa shared a room in their aunt's house, and as Louisa was even more prickly when denied her desired amount of beauty sleep, she was determined not to wake her. Clutching her writing case to her chest, she crept into the parlour and was surprised to find her mother already there, sitting bundled up in a chair close to the embers of the fire.

"Mama!" Juliet's cry was louder and seemed louder still in the quiet of the house. She cringed, dropping her voice to a whisper, and hurried to her mother's side. "Is something the matter? You are not still unwell, are you?"

"Oh, no!" Mrs Turner smiled, patting the empty chair next to her and silently inviting her daughter to join her. "I was just awake, probably because I spent so long sleeping yesterday. I could not abide lying still any longer and have been trying to read, but I confess my thoughts are so eager to run amok that I struggle to keep pace with a novel." She closed the book that had lain open, unread, on her lap and turned to Juliet. "But why are you awake so early?"

"I thought to write," Juliet began, clutching her writing case as proof of her intent. "But I much prefer to speak to you." She dropped a kiss on her mother's cheek, feeling a strange stab of sadness at the distance that would unavoidably come between them, once she and Edmund were married. It had happened with Maddy, and it would with Bess. An overwhelming sense of the loss her mother had weathered in a few short months swept over Juliet, and as she settled into her chair she turned to look at her mother carefully, seeing for the first lines around her eyes that suggested her age.

"Mama…" She could not quite think how to put into words the concern she felt, but somehow Mrs Turner seemed to sense it, all the same, reaching over and taking Juliet's hand in hers.

"I am not sure I have had a chance to properly tell you how happy I am that you and Edmund are to be married." She squeezed Juliet's hand and smiled. "I confess, it is what I wished for since I first saw how close a friendship existed between you." Her eyes sparkled with amusement. "I should never have spoken of it, of course, for to do so would be to turn you in entirely the opposite direction."

Juliet smiled, despite herself.

"You have always known your mind and not cared to be advised or directed in any way." She let out a low sigh. "You and Louisa are both alike in that."

"Louisa?" Juliet sniffed. "We are not alike at all, Mother, how can you say so?" She tugged on one of her tangled curls, pulling a droll face. "Can you imagine Miss Fashion-Plate ever emerging from her room without her hair perfectly in place, clad for style instead of for warmth?" She pulled a worn but comfortable shawl a little tighter around her shoulders, shivering for effect. "No, Mama, you are mistaken there. Louisa and I are not alike at all!"

Mrs Turner said nothing, but her eyebrows lifted as if she did not quite agree with Juliet's assessment. Changing the subject, she released her hold on Juliet's hand and tapped her writing case.

"Tell me about your book. What has become of poor Isabella and her Count?"

"Oh, they will marry, of course," Juliet said, airily. She launched into a vivid description of the duel the anguished Count Valentino had been forced to undertake to secure his bride, and the villainy of her father in seeking to prevent the match, instead betrothing her to another.

"I had thought to have them run away together, throwing off the shackles of obligation and expectation and be happy -"

Mrs Turner sucked in a breath, and Juliet hurried to reassure her.

"But I did not!" She smiled. "There shall be no such scandal in my pages, Mama, do not fret. No matter how romantic I think it might be." She let out a sigh, before shaking off the notion. "No, my hero will win over Isabella's father in some great feat of daring heroism, and he will be so enamoured with him he will consent to the marriage on the spot."

"I suppose, the fact that he is a Count has been of some assistance in this?" Mrs Turner's lips quirked, for she always took great amusement in the adventures that befell her daughter's characters.

"A *penniless* count," Juliet interposed. "If he had wealth as well as a title, what obstacle could there be?" She laughed. "I dare say it is foolish, and no publisher will ever care to see it, but it has given me so much enjoyment to scribble away that I do not even mind. I have written of ordinary folk, and I have written of adventure and I confess at present I prefer the latter, however unlikely it will ever be to be printed."

"You should submit it, all the same," Mrs Turner said, her voice growing determined. "If it is rejected, it is rejected. You must not merely place it in a drawer and forget about it." She turned to her daughter with an earnest expression on her face. "Promise me, Juliet, that no matter how happy you are when you and Edmund are married - and I do hope and pray you are happy - you will not abandon your dreams, simply because other people might think them foolish."

"I won't, Mama," Juliet managed, at last, surprised to see such feeling in her usually sanguine mother's expression.

A floorboard creaked overhead, and both ladies glanced reflexively upwards, a slight sigh escaping Mrs Turner's lips. "I suppose our hostess will be upon us before very much longer. I am sure your aunt will rejoice in the drama and scandal in your pages, Juliet. Perhaps do not tell her that you have placed just as much focus on morality as you have on excitement, for she will not favour that half so much."

Her expression seemed strangely sad to Juliet, and she reached out a hand to her mother's arm, but Mrs Turner shook it off.

"Do not worry about me, my dear. I have known my brother's sister longer than you have been alive. Known her before she was Mrs Brierley, even! But we have never quite been friendly. There is very little alike in our characters, and I wager she did not much rate me as a sister." Her eyes sparkled. "Yet sisters we are, after a fashion, and we have learned to tolerate one another." Her expression softened. "You will find, my dear, that family opposition can and does relent over time." She dropped a comforting kiss on Juliet's forehead and stood.

"Well, I will leave you to your writing. I imagine you have a great deal to do before preparations begin for the assembly. I shall see you at breakfast, dear."

"Goodbye, Mama," Juliet replied, turning to watch her mother glide gracefully from the room. She could not help but think of Mrs Gale and take some comfort from her mother's words. She must persevere with Edmund's mother, and in time, they would find some way to bear being around one another. She bit her lip, thinking she might manage the task all the better if Mrs Gale were a little more like Aunt Brierley!

Smiling at the thought, she flipped open her writing case and shuffled through her papers, trying to recall where last she left off, and plunging herself back into a great, dramatic duel with abandon. *How much easier such conflicts become on the page!* The thought of challenging Edmund's staid, simpering Mama to a duel tickled her, and she smiled as she wrote, scarcely noticing the passage of time.

MRS GALE HAD SOFTENED a little towards Edmund ever since their call at the Grenvilles. He did not think it likely that her opinion of Juliet had changed at all, but he dared to hope that she was at least softening to the fact of his marriage, and had come to accept that his choice had been made.

"How well you look, Mama!" he exclaimed, coming into the parlour the evening of the assembly and finding, to his surprise, that she was sitting there waiting for him. "And look, we are both ready early this evening!"

Mrs Gale stood, walking over to him and adjusting his cravat as if he were far younger than his years.

"This evening shall be far more widely attended than the assemblies we are used to at home; it is only sensible to aim to arrive early if we wish to have any chance of seeing our friends."

Edmund smiled, cheered to see his mother more like her old self than she had been for many weeks.

"I suppose you shall want to wait for Juliet and the rest of the Turners, even if we arrive before them?"

Edmund's smile stretched, but he nodded, determined not to allow his mother to bait him before the evening was even begun.

"You suppose right, but I shall not force you to do the same." He leaned free of her hold, tugging the cravat himself and undoing all her good work, and following that up with a rumple of his dark curls for good measure. "You shall know plenty enough people there that I am sure you'll be pleased to be rid of me."

Mrs Gale looked at him, her expression almost wistful, and Edmund wondered if he had said the wrong thing. He smiled, to show that he was teasing, but her expression did not change.

"I think if either of us will be pleased to be rid of one another it shall be you." She smiled, and when she did the expression was so tragic that Edmund felt himself drawn back to her side, fearing that some great calamity had befallen her that he was as-yet unaware of. He said nothing, though, and after a moment she blinked what looked like tears out of her eyes and drew in a stilted breath. "I am sure you will be so happy with your new bride that you shall scarcely even notice my absence! No, come along, if you are ready, and we shall be on our way."

"Mama?" Edmund asked, holding out a hand to stop her as she made her way towards the door.

"We have no time, Edmund -"

"We have plenty of time, Mama." He frowned, stern but gentle. "We could spare a few moments to speak freely with one another, without an audience." He gestured towards a long, low-backed chaise and sat down on it, waiting with bated breath until she joined him.

"I do not know what we need to speak to one another about..." she mused, her voice sliding easily back into that airy, don't-care attitude she had used with him of late.

"I know you do not approve of Juliet and my intent to marry, Mama. You have made your position clear. I know it is not *Juliet* that you dislike, nor the Turners, for they were our neighbours and friends all my life. Papa considered Mr Turner a friend, and I know that you did not dislike them. You regret, then, that I made my own choice, and did not bend to your will in this? Would you have been happier if I had married Miss Drew or another just like her?"

Mrs Gale fixed him with an unblinking stare, and Edmund did not look away, determined that they should have it out now, and be done with the matter once and for all.

"Would you?"

"No," his mother said at last. "I confess it was pride on my part to think that I knew you better than you knew yourself, that I might find you a bride more deserving of your brilliance." She lifted a hand to smooth down the curls that would forever rumple and refuse to lie flat. "I thought you deserved more..."

She paused, her hand dropping to her lap, where she folded it with its companion and stared down at them, as if not quite sure she could bring herself to speak the whole.

"And?" Edmund prompted, watching her carefully for any clue she might offer even beyond words.

"Juliet is such a strong-willed young lady. She has never borne advice well, nor sought it out. When you marry - when she is the mistress of Northridge, what place will that leave me? You shan't need me any more, and she will resent me being there, and -" Her voice shook and she bit her lip, evidently not trusting herself to say any more.

"Mama!" Edmund laughed, then, seeing that she was serious, swallowed his amusement. "Mama, if you think Juliet would wish you gone from your own home then you do not know her at all. And she is strong-willed, yes, but do you see her keeping a home? She will need you to guide her, to show her all that is required of the mistress of Northridge." He ducked his head, attempting to catch her eye. "I wish you would take more time to get to know her. She is not as confident as you think, and she despairs of me at least as much as you do." He grinned. "I dare say you could develop quite a friendship, bonding over your shared exasperations at my many flaws."

Mrs Gale looked at him tenderly, before letting out a long, low sigh.

"I suppose you are not mistaken there. I must thank her, for instance, for pressing you to come to London and bring me with you." She looked around their elegant parlour with a sigh of satisfaction. "I do adore this house, and have been here so rarely since your father's death…"

"I know." Edmund slipped his hand into his Mama's and squeezed it. "And you forever pleaded to be brought, if only I had listened. Perhaps we shall go on better together, now, if we listen to one another more."

Mrs Gale smiled, and together mother and son made their way out into the light, London evening, feeling as if a great many more truths had been shared than were spoken aloud in their short conversation.

Chapter Nine

Strolling into the assembly rooms with Abigail on his arm, and in tow to his aunt, Nash could not help but recall the last such gathering he had attended, and how different the Castleford assembly rooms had been to these.

"Good evening, Weston!"

He turned at this address, greeting an older gentleman with a smile and a wave, and grateful that his aunt had moved on ahead of him, bidding him continue, for he could not for the life of him remember the stranger's name and did not wish to embarrass himself by asking it.

"There are so many people here!" Abigail exclaimed, her eyes wide. She clutched rather desperately at Nash, enhancing his trapped feeling, and he felt a fleeting desire to wrench himself free and walk away. It would be impolite, though, not to mention unkind. It was hardly Abigail's fault that their aunt had matched the pair from the time that they were babies. She had been as trapped by this arrangement as he had been. Clearing his throat, he tried to be kind and also did his best to put a little more distance between them, though it meant holding his arm at quite an unnatural and uncomfortable angle for a moment.

"Do you see anyone you know? There are certain to be friends here and I do not wish to keep you from meeting them."

Abigail shook her head, blinking rather stupidly.

"I am quite sure I know no-one! All of London is new to me, you see -"

"That can't be true," Nash protested, thinking of how often he had had cause to be in town, whether or not he had been summoned there to see his aunt. "Surely you just mean that it has been some time since your last visit."

"Oh indeed!" She nodded her head, seriously. "Quite some time. I believe I was...four years old when last I accompanied Mother and Father." She bit her lip. "They died soon after, you see, and I was sent away to school. I have lived quietly in the countryside ever since!"

Nash was silent for a moment, seeking to find some other topic of conversation with which to engage his companion. This was the greatest number of words he had ever heard corm from her thin lips and he did not wish for them to lapse back into an awkward, uneasy silence.

"The countryside is quite charming, too," he said. "I am fond of it myself, the walking, shooting..."

"That is why you remained so long at Northridge."

It was not quite a question, but Nash felt a strange compulsion to reply.

"Yes. I enjoyed spending time with my friends."

"Does Mr Gale have brothers and sisters?" Abigail asked, looking at him with what, on some other lady, might have been a canny expression.

He frowned, curious as to the origin of her question.

"You say you enjoyed spending time with *friends*. I merely assumed that there were more people at Northridge than Mr Gale and his mother."

"There were at first," Nash explained. "A group of us travelled down, but I remained even after the others had returned to their own homes."

"Until you could stay no longer without aggravating out aunt," Abigail suggested, with a sanguine smile. "Yes, I see that she was very effective in summoning you back."

"I came because Edmund wished to come to London," Nash said, shortly. "I could not very well stay in his house without him."

"And yet, for such close friends, you have scarcely seen him since you arrived in London. Why is that, I wonder?"

Nash bristled, rather inclined to think he preferred Abigail when she was too meek to say a word. He had thought her insipid, now he wondered if she was objectionable, too.

"Nash!"

As if the fleeting mention of his name had summoned him into being, Edmund himself crossed the room, dodging expertly past groups of gathering friends, his face lit up with a broad, friendly smile. Instantly Nash felt at ease and forsook Abigail to shake his friend's hand with all the warmth he could muster.

"Edmund! Are you well?"

"Indeed, yes! And you have come. How splendid, Mama will be pleased. And Louisa will be delighted. She has been a little out of sorts since the family's arrival, so between us, we must work to cheer her this evening...." He trailed off, noticing, for the first time, that his old friend was not alone. He dropped in a bow, greeting Abigail politely and turning to Nash with an amiable smile to encourage an introduction.

"Miss Carter, this is my friend, Mr Edmund Gale. Ed, may I present Miss Carter, my c-"

"Fiancée," she offered, clutching hold of Nash's hand, almost before he realised it was free. "Yes, I know we had not yet planned to tell everyone, darling, but I do not think I can keep the secret any longer. Your aunt has already begun to introduce me as such, and it seems silly to keep it from people who are such close friends of yours - of *ours*." She beamed at Edmund a little too widely Edmund's smile dimmed considerably.

"Fiancée?" His glance shifted to Nash, as if expecting the whole to have been a joke, but Nash could find no words to either confirm or counter Abigail's confession. He swallowed past a lump in his throat and spotted his aunt, bustling over to them with enthusiastic speed.

"You are not yet acquainted with my aunt, either, I believe. Aunt Reed, this is Edmund Gale, recall, the friend I told you about."

"The friend who kept you so long that the rest of us feared we never would see you again!" His aunt said, with a cool nod. "Pleased to know you, Mr Gale, and I gather I am to congratulate you on your own recent engagement. Nash, do let me steal Miss Carter away a moment. There is somebody I am eager for her to meet. Come along my dear, you shall have time enough to hang on my nephew's arm once the dancing begins!"

The two ladies hurried away and Nash felt his shoulders sag noticeably the instant they were out of sight. He would have faded away completely, were it not for the heavy hand Edmund clamped on his shoulder, forcing him to remain upright and to look at him. His features were stiff and serious, not at all like the friendly, affable young man he ordinarily was.

"We must have a conversation, Nash, before the celebrations begin. Let's step outside a moment, while everyone is still arriving. You look pale as a ghost, and shall need some livening up if you intend to dance this evening."

Nash allowed his friend to steer him out of doors, disappointment giving way to a strange sense of relief now that the secret was out, the truth spoken. His friend would lecture him, no doubt, for his behaviour. He had been cruel and now he was paying a penance. The engagement offer may not have been made by him in as many words, but it was as good as arranged now. *If I had the chance to escape, it is lost to me now. There is nothing to do but go through with it.*

The night air was cool, but not cold, for summer was well and truly upon the town, and Nash inhaled the sickly-sweet scent of jasmine as he and Edmund wound their way past crowds of newly-arrived guests, nodding and smiling to those they recognised as they passed.

"Edmund?"

Nash recognised Juliet's voice and before he could turn away the whole Turner party greeted them, along with the older, stouter lady he recognised from the day of the lecture, and another, slighter man who must be her husband. He turned to leave, hoping to fade into the crowd, but Edmund caught hold of his sleeve, holding him fast with the tiniest glance.

"It is very kind od you to come out to greet us, Mr Gale, but I assure you quite unnecessary!" Juliet's aunt said, beaming and blushing, nonetheless, at such a warm and welcome reception from not one but two handsome young gentlemen. "And who is your friend?"

"This is Mr Weston, Mrs Reed."

Nash was forced to look up, his eyes locking for the first and last time on Louisa. She looked particularly pretty that evening, just as he remembered, only more vibrant, more alive than his memory gave credence to. His mouth was dry and when he opened it to greet them he could conjure not a single word of greeting. Instead, his desire to flee overcame him and he wrenched his arm free of Edmund's clutches, dipping his head in a vague sort of bow and disappearing into the crowd without a backward glance.

"WELL! I CALL THAT QUITE rude!"

Aunt Reed had declared Nash *quite rude* above a handful of times and every time she did it was like a dagger to Louisa's heart. There was no pretending, now. Nash was not playing a game with her, he had not mistaken her for a stranger or failed to see her at all. He had looked directly at her, smiled a little, at least she thought she had, just enough to cause her hopes to rise just a little all the more cruelly to be dashed when he turned and fled from her as if from a firing squad.

Louisa kept her head down, no longer eager to see the dresses worn by elegant London ladies, nor to admire the tall ceilings and shaped cornices of the building her uncle had rhapsodised over on their way here. She was not quick enough to avoid the helpless look exchanged between Juliet and Edmund, and when he offered his arm to *her* and not to his fiancée, Louisa's face flamed with embarrassment. She took it, unable to think of a suitable refusal, and lifted her head as he escorted her into the room, chattering ten-to-the-dozen as if to distract her. She scarcely heard a word, though, her eyes scanning the crowd. It took her a moment to realise she was looking for someone, and a moment longer to realise she was looking for *Nash*. She bit her lip and looked down, wondering just how foolish she must be to still want to see him after being so pointedly snubbed.

He was not like that before! She wanted to scream the words aloud, to explain to everyone she passed that she was not a foolish little wallflower, easily swayed by a few sweet words and handsome smiles.

Was it this, then, that hurt her more than Nash himself? She had been misled. *She*! Louisa Turner, the most beautiful and petted of all her sisters. She had been destined for greatness and certain that, when her time came, she would have scores of suitors and be able to marry precisely as she chose. Now it seemed she was deemed only worthy of games from a gentleman who had no intention of ever marrying her, if he even thought to see her again.

I thought he cared for me. This, then, was the shame of it all. She had believed his affections to be genuine and they had been proved false, in the most public and humiliating of ways.

Juliet will never let me forget this! Her cheeks flamed with heat. Her sister was always lecturing her for thinking too much of her appearance and what had been her constant defence? *It will net me a handsome suitor and a wealthy one, so I shall pay my appearance all the attention I care to, thank you very much!* How their roles had been reversed! Juliet was the one with the handsome, accomplished, wealthy suitor and she - Louisa - had been utterly abandoned.

"Louisa?"

It took a second prompting for her to realise that Edmund was speaking to her and she looked up at him, blinking rapidly as she was returned with haste to the present.

"Sorry! My thoughts - ran away with me." She swallowed past the lump in her throat and met Edmund's gaze, defying him to look on her with pity. He didn't, but smiled, in that same mischievous way that spoke to her of home, and reminded her of the many enjoyable times they had had together over the years.

"I suppose I should not expect you to listen to an old, soon-to-married man like me." He sighed, in a gesture of disappointment. "Well, I shall not monopolise you any more, for you are sure to find a better partner than I could ever be." He stepped back from her then, exchanging a glance with a shy-looking fellow to her right, and Louisa accepted his fumbling offer to dance with her. He was not Nash, but he would do. She dazzled him with her most brilliant smile, causing him to fumble as they found their places amongst the other dancers. Louisa glanced over her shoulder to see Edmund and Juliet settle behind her, their heads bent together in a whisper that surely concerned her.

Snapping her eyes back to her partner, she tried to put all thought of them from her mind. Let them pity her if they dared to. She would show them, this evening, that she was in no need of pity. She would show Nash, too, precisely how little she cared to have lost his good opinion and affection if, indeed, she had ever had them to begin with.

Chapter Ten

Nash stood to attention by his aunt's chair, his back ramrod straight, watching the dancers. Watching *one* dancer in particular. There was Louisa, dancing with Edmund this time, and both of them were smiling and laughing as if they had not a care in the world. His heart ached. How he wished *he* could be the one who whispered something to her that made her laugh and cover her face with one hand for fear of betraying herself. The eyes of every other gentleman in their circle was drawn to Louisa, it seemed to him, and Nash was certainly not the only observer who was taken with the pretty fair-haired young lady who moved with such grace and charm.

"Nash, I appreciate your determination to keep me company," Mrs Reed said, not turning to look at him. "But I do not need a permanent guard. Surely you would much rather dance. Where is Abigail?"

"We have already danced several times together, Aunt. Indeed, it was she who requested we sit one dance out." He glanced around, then, realising for the first time that Abigail was not beside them. He spotted her in a moment, perched at a table with two other young ladies whispering, a malicious smile occasionally darting onto her face.

This was the same Abigail who knew nobody in London? His lips quirked. Had that been a fabrication? Or was she, perhaps, excessively talented at befriending strangers? Either tale did not seem to match the picture of his cousin he held in his mind.

"Perhaps you would care to ask another young lady to dance, in that case," his aunt suggested, in a tone that brooked no disagreement. "It is the responsibility of any true gentleman to offer young ladies a chance to dance - listen, the musicians are stopping, so your timing is perfect. Perhaps -"

But Nash did not hear what his aunt had to say next. He was striding across the room, his gaze fixed on Louisa. This was his only opportunity, and he would seize it, now.

"Thank you, Miss Louisa!" Edmund was laughing, hiccupping through his words.

"Thank you, Mr Gale." Louisa pulled a face at him, dropping in a curtsy. "Now go and dance with Juliet again. I can see from here she is getting agitated over there in her corner, and will doubtless cause someone offence..."

Edmund glanced around, seeing and understanding the issue in a moment. He took off like a shot, intervening on behalf of his increasingly frustrated fiancée and suggesting that she might like to work off a little of her annoyance by dancing with him.

"Miss Louisa." Nash had slipped into the very space Edmund had vacated, dropping in a quick bow before straightening and fixing his eyes on Louisa's.

Her eyes widened momentarily in surprise at seeing him before she drew her lips into a line.

"Mr Weston," she said, flatly.

"I wonder if I might have the next dance."

Louisa glanced at the musicians, a delaying tactic, Nash was sure.

"Actually, I was thinking to sit down..."

"Then perhaps you will allow me to accompany you -"

"But as you have asked so politely, I suppose it would only be right to accept." She looked back at him again, her blue eyes flashing with something that might have been anger or pain. "Unless you prefer to dance with your fiancée?"

Nash swallowed, trying desperately to cobble together the words that would get him out of this mess, that would undo the hurt he had so evidently caused this pretty, charming young lady who had done nothing but be sweet to him.

"She is otherwise occupied. I would much rather dance with you, and perhaps it will afford me a chance to explain."

Louisa arched an eyebrow, looking in that one gesture of disdain so like Juliet that he almost remarked upon it. Before he could say another word, though, the music had begun again and they were forced to take their place amongst the other dancers and begin.

Once dancing, Nash began to rethink the wisdom of his actions. He had longed for an opportunity to speak to Louisa, to explain things, and now that he had it, he found he had no notion of what to say. What explanation could he give that would undo this?

"How do you like London, Miss Louisa?"

Louisa winced, evidently noticing, as he did, the unfamiliar "Miss" that had dropped away so easily when they were together at Aston House.

"I wonder that you sought to be away from it so long!" she retorted, her eyes turned away from him as she spoke. "If I had a fiancée I loved and an aunt to welcome me, I am not sure I would have cared to be absent for longer than was necessary." She did not say, *nor forming attachments with other young ladies*, but the accusation was there all the same.

"If I had a fiancée I loved and an aunt who did not hold me hostage, perhaps I would not have wished to escape, either."

He had spoken these words aloud almost before he was aware of having thought them, and Louisa looked up at him in surprise and alarm, startled by his honesty.

"I oughtn't to have said that," he muttered, as the dance permitted them to pass one another close enough that they might speak freely without fear of being overheard.

"Because it is not true?"

Something in Louisa's tone of voice, in her eyes as she looked at him, was so filled with feeling and hope - two things that were so long missing from Nash's life that he found himself answering honestly, little caring of propriety.

"Because it is not gentlemanly." His lips quirked. "It is not kind."

"I would suggest deception is *less* kind," Louisa commented, shooting him the same kind of regal, imperious look that had first captured his heart. Life was so simple for Louisa Turner. How could she begin to understand the obligations that were placed on him?

"I did not deceive you, Louisa. At least, I did not mean to." He paused, waiting for the dance to bring them closer again to continue his confession without their closest dancing neighbours as an audience. "I wished to escape a future laid out for me by another. I wish..." He shrugged his shoulders, summing up all of his regret in one slight motion. "I wanted to imagine life could be different, that I could marry as I chose and be happy." He dropped his gaze. "I am sorry that you were hurt, but I never did deceive you about my affections. One's heart is different from one's duty, and my heart was lost to you from our first meeting."

"I SHALL KILL HIM," Juliet muttered. "I shall trip him up and ensure he falls flat on his obnoxiously handsome face."

"You shall do no such thing," Edmund said, soothingly. "And is he so very handsome?"

Juliet eyed her betrothed with irritation.

"Regardless," Edmund continued, pretending not to notice the look. "It is right and proper he should explain himself to Louisa. Better he does it here, in a crowd -"

"With witnesses, you mean," Juliet hissed, balling her hands into fists, one of which Edmund struggled to grasp at the next point in their dance, and he tapped it gently, a reminder to her to uncoil and allow the dance to play out.

"We do not know the entire story," he reminded her. "Perhaps, after this, we may begin to learn it."

"I do not care to learn anything!" Juliet sniffed. "Did you see how stricken Louisa looked to see him on our arrival? And the way he looked right through her, as if she were not even there? It was abominable-"

"I happen to know that you have deployed the self-same method of expressing your annoyance with a gentleman not a million miles from you at this moment," Edmund said, patiently, smiling to recall the numerous falling outs that had taken place between them during their long and winding road to courtship.

"That was different" Juliet insisted. "You deserved it!!"

He shot her a contrite look and she softened, smiling as the dance forced them to part momentarily. Reunited a moment later, she let out a sigh and conceded him the point.

"Very well, I suppose you are right and it is good that they might speak." Her lips quirked. "At least I can trust Louisa to guard her heart. Of all of my sisters, she is the surest of her own mind. I do not like Nash's chances of winning her to his cause a second time. He has hurt her and she does not forgive easily."

"I wonder who in her family she shares that trait with," Edmund mused, shooting his bride-to-be a look that was both affectionate and teasing.

Juliet returned her attention to a couple a little way in front of them. It was one thing for Edmund to tease and be charming, but at that moment she was more concerned with his friend. Nash had won Louisa's heart - had won all of their hears - so easily, she feared his ability to talk himself out of the trouble he rightly deserved to be in.

At least now I understand poor Louisa's peculiarity of late, she thought. She had done her sister a disservice, thinking that proud, pretty Louisa scarcely even possessed a heart, much less had lost it to their neighbour's handsome guest. She had taken their friendship for an amusing distraction, one that was equal parts performance and self-interest, for it pleased Louisa to have secured the attentions of so charming a gentleman and she flourished. It had never occurred to her that there was any real feeling there.

capable of meting out." Her smile grew. "I do not envy him the consequences of crossing Louisa Turner."

Chapter Eleven

My *heart was lost to you from our first meeting.* Louisa repeated Nash's words over and over in her mind as she stood by her aunt, ostensibly watching the other dancers, but in reality, playing and replaying the one dance she and Nash had shared, revisiting every word he had said and mining it for value.

"There is that handsome Mr Weston," her aunt remarked, and Louisa flinched, fearing for a moment that she had betrayed herself. She followed the line of her aunt's gaze, though, and saw, indeed, that there was Nash, escorting his fiancée - how her heart ached to think of it! - towards his aunt's table. He bowed to both ladies and turned, meeting Louisa's gaze for the briefest of moments.

"Here, auntie, you must be tired of standing in one spot. Shall we sit?"

"I suppose that is wise," Mrs Brierley said, with a sigh. "Although I refuse to have you join me." She tucked a stray curl behind Louisa's ear and patted her warmly on the shoulder.

"You have had enough rest from dancing and humoured me like the delightful niece you are. Now, go and enjoy yourself! The evening will not last forever!"

Louisa smiled, watching as her aunt melted into the crowd. She turned back to the dancers, wondering if she would be asked again but a figure barged past her so suddenly they struck her shoulder. She turned to admonish them, when she noticed the figure had dropped something into her hand as she passed. She glanced up, recognising Nash's back, and bent over the note, unrolling it and reading it as quickly as she could without being noticed.

Meet me on the terrace.

The terrace? Louisa was torn. There was something risky in following a gentleman - one she knew to be engaged! - on some sort of secret assignation. But the terrace was quite well lit and public. It could surely be no worse than dancing with the man, and nobody had objected to that. Biting her lip, she took one last look around the room to assure herself that she was not being observed, before stepping quickly towards the door, tearing Nash's hurried note into scraps she disposed of as she walked.

"Louisa! Where are you off to in such a hurry?"

Colonel Brierley was red-faced and merry, and at first, Louisa feared he would delay her or prevent her from going altogether. His gaze was unfocused, and he beamed at her.

"Lovely evening, isn't it?"

"It is, Uncle," Louisa said, slipping towards the door. "I am a little over-heated after all the dancing. I am just going to take a little air."

"Ah, yes. Indeed." He frowned. "Do you wish for me to escort you?"

"No!" Louisa's rejection was so sudden, she hurried to temper it with a smile. "You are very kind, but I shall just take a short walk along the terrace. Look, I see a group of young ladies

I am acquainted with. I will stop and pass a word or two with them and then return."

This excuse might not have passed muster with either her parents or her aunt, but Colonel Brierley was unused to the reasonings of young ladies and far too inebriated to make a sensible judgment. He nodded and even went so far as to open the door for her.

"I hope to see you dancing again before long, my dear!" he called, his voice loud in the quiet of the night.

The group of young ladies that Louisa had mentioned giggled at his intrusion, before glancing significantly at Louisa and moving away. She might have taken offence at such a snub from strangers but at this moment her whole attention was fixed on her reason for being here.

"Nash?" she murmured, peering into the shadows to see if she might spy him. She did spy others, pairs and groups of young ladies and gentlemen seeking a little more calm and privacy than the great assembly hall allowed, but no Nash. She was poised to abandon her search, carving up another folly at the feet of her old friend, when Nash appeared to her right, offering her his arm and, when she took it, leading them both to a deserted part of the terrace. Louisa glanced over her shoulder towards the door but satisfied herself that she could still both see and hear other revellers.

"I am glad you came." Nash grinned. "And that you received my note."

"Yes." Louisa frowned, rubbing the shoulder he had barged into. "You needn't have been quite so violent in the passing of it!"

"Poor lamb." He lifted her hand to his lips and kissed it. "I am sorry, but I was eager to have the matter done. It is quite a risk we are taking, meeting like this."

"Yes, so say what must be said and have done with it," Louisa said, her heart beating hard in her chest. This was the Nash she recalled from home, charming, adventurous and fun, yet with all that had happened in the last few days, Louisa was not quite sure she could trust him.

"I have already said some," he began, his voice low and gentle. "I told you I loved you, and I do. I cannot bear to be apart from you."

"And yet you are to marry another." Louisa's voice rang with bitterness and she glanced over her shoulder, fearful at having been overheard.

"It was not my choice," Nash replied, seeking to soften her mood. "And the engagement was as much news to me as it was to you."

"What do you mean?" Louisa was confused, massaging her head which had begun to ache. The tiny lie she had told her uncle of growing overheated in the assembly room seemed to be coming true.

"It was aunt's plan that I marry Miss Carter, but no offer had been made - not on my part, at least. This evening they are acting as if all has been agreed, yet I do not recall ever making such an offer. How could I? My heart belongs to another."

Louisa shivered, partly from the cold and partly at hearing the words she had begun to fear she never would hear, on Nash Weston's lips. *My heart was lost to you from our first meeting.*

"But there is no way out." She had indulged the dream for only a moment, before her rational self had hold of her once more. "You must marry her."

"I must, if I seek to have my inheritance," Nash muttered, casting his gaze down. He lifted his eyes to hers a moment later. "And yet, at this moment, I find I care less for my inheritance than I thought. Less for my aunt's interference. That she would go so far as to announce a theoretical someday engagement as a present fact has proved she cares little for me or my happiness: truly she wishes only to manipulate me into doing as she wishes, and if I am miserable, then I shall be miserable." His eyes glowed with a fierce intensity. "I do not care to be miserable, Louisa. I care to be happy. With you. If you will have me."

"WOULD YOU NOT PREFER to dance than sit and entertain an old married man?"

Mr Turner's voice was weary, but there was a sparkle in his eyes that suggested humour.

"I am an old married man myself, these days, or soon will be!" Edmund retorted, rearranging his cards to best survey what they held. "And I have danced plenty." He winced, trying to ignore the ache in his feet and wondering whether it was synonymous with engagement to feel all of a sudden as if one had aged a decade.

"I shall not complain about your company, in that case." Mr Turner smirked and played his hand. "Particularly not when it affords me such an easy win. Perhaps, Mr Gale, you have left your brains at Northridge?"

"I am merely encouraging you to let down your guard," Edmund remarked, rueing the easy error that had cost him the game. "Let us play another hand and you shall see where I have left my brains!"

A riot of musical laughter behind him caught Edmund's ear as he dealt and he turned, surveying the crowd to locate his mother, and thinking it had been quite some time since last he had seen her. For a moment, his heart caught in his chest as he located her with her friends all surrounding his fiancée. He was poised to leap from his chair and intercede, rescuing Juliet from whatever fate his mother had subjected her to and already meditating on the lecture he would deliver, when Mr Turner cleared his throat, drawing Edmund's attention momentarily back to their game. Juliet's father was nonchalantly arranging his cards, his eyes ostensibly fixed on them, but when he spoke it was clear he had witnessed just what Edmund had, and drawn his own conclusions.

"It appears my daughter has secured quite an audience of admirers, of whom your mother is chief. Perhaps she left something of her own at Northridge."

Edmund peered back over his shoulder, his concern melting as he read the situation correctly this time, marvelling at how Juliet held court, discussing the lecture she had attended and - no, he was not dreaming - Mama was clutching hold of Juliet's hand and declaring to her friends that her soon-to-be daughter was writing a novel of her own. She beamed with pride that could not have been more genuine if she was talking about her own daughter.

Smiling to himself, his eyebrows lifted in surprise at this strange turn of events, he returned to the matter at hand, and he and Mr Turner fell to their game. Whatever he had said to his mother that evening had worked, for she appeared to have left all her resentment behind and began to treat Juliet as he had once hoped she would. *How much easier life will become, once the two are friends!*

He identified Juliet's laughter, then, in unison with Mama's, and when he glanced back he was surprised to find himself the recipient of several pairs of eyes.

"Ah, and this is perhaps the *less* exciting result of one's female family members uniting." Mr Turner's eyebrows wiggled in amusement. "They tend to find they have a common enemy."

Edmund frowned, not quite sure he approved of this. He played on in silence for a moment, until their game was disturbed by the arrival of another lady known to them both.

"My dear! I wondered where you had got to. Come, sit with us and watch me defeat Edmund twice in as many games."

"Thank you, no," Mrs Turner said, shooting Edmund a polite but distracted smile. "I was looking for Louisa. I do not suppose you have seen her?"

"Louisa?" Edmund straightened, casting about for some sign of her. The last he had seen her was dancing with Nash, although he could see his friend, once more trapped in a stark circle with his aunt and fiancée. *Fiancée.* The word still rankled. Not that Nash had one, for he could scarcely begrudge any fellow that, but that he had kept her existence a secret. It seemed to be an unhappy pattern with his friends, of concealing obligations in one place to allow them the freedom to act as they pleased in another. His hand itched and he scratched it, absent-mindedly laying his next card. He had only been half-serious when he suggested to Juliet that he might call Nash out for his caddish actions, but he could not help but feel the desire for some recompense. The man needed dressing down, and if not in public then in private. Edmund vowed to speak to him and not let him escape without reprimand.

"I am sure she is here somewhere, my dear," Mr Turner replied, surprisingly unconcerned with the whereabouts of his youngest daughter. "You know how she is at assemblies. She can hardly bear to be with her family." He smiled, drolly, and played his move. "Do you recall, at Castleford -"

"This is not Castleford!" Mrs Turner responded, so sharply that both gentlemen looked at her in concern. "Forgive me," she murmured, dabbing at her neck with a lace-trimmed handkerchief. "My nerves are a little on edge on account of the heat."

She had scarcely finished speaking when Edmund leapt from his seat, pleading with her to take it. The movement had attracted the attention of the ladies, once more, and Juliet succeeded in freeing herself from Mrs Gale's clutches to come and see what was the matter.

"Juliet!" Mrs Turner grasped her hand as her daughter came close. "Where is your sister?"

"Louisa?" Juliet looked at Edmund, who shrugged his shoulders, dropping his cards down on the table. He straightened, offering his arm to his fiancée.

"Shall we go and find her? Stay here, both of you, and we shall not return alone!"

"Don't worry, Mama," Juliet counselled her, as Edmund escorted her towards the door, scanning the crowds as he went for Louisa's familiar blonde curls.

"Where is Mr Weston?" Juliet cried, as soon as they were far enough away from her parents that they could be confident of not being overheard. "If he has -"

"He has done nothing," Edmund soothed her. "I see him now, over with his aunt and..." He paused. "With his aunt. And anyway, you and I both watched him and Louisa dance together and part without disaster." He smiled. "I daresay your sister has forgotten the slight and set her heart on a more worthy fellow." He guided her towards the dining room, a sudden inspiration striking him that a great many young men doted on ladies by procuring them refreshments. In this instance, his idea was fruitless, for, whilst they saw and greeted a great many friends and acquaintances, they did not see Louisa, and could not abandon their search in favour of polite conversation.

"Where is she?" Juliet's voice quavered and Edmund forced a smile, determined to reassure her, although he could not offer the answer she so desperately longed for.

"Juliet! Edmund! There you are!"

Mrs Brierley was standing to one side, speaking with a friend of hers, another broad, greying lady bedecked with finery. "I suppose you have come to find me, for it is time our party made for home." She sighed. "You see what it is coming to when even the young people are ready to go home at such an hour as this."

"No, Auntie," Juliet hurried, glancing at Edmund. "We are looking for Louisa. Have you seen her?"

"Louisa?" Mrs Brierley cackled from behind her fan. "What is my mischievous young niece up to now? Are you sure she is not dancing? My niece, Mrs Whipple, is quite the most graceful dancer I have ever seen. And her hair shines so beautifully in the candlelight as she moves. Why, I would be quite jealous of her if I were younger..."

"You have not seen her, then?" Edmund asked, forestalling yet more raptures of Louisa's beauty that ordinarily would have provoked amusement in him.

"I have not - Oh, look! There she is!" Mrs Brierley lifted her fan, waving over the heads of several other guests to attract Louisa's attention.

Juliet let go of Edmund and scurried forward, digging her fingers into Louisa's arm in a way that made Edmund wince.

"Where have you been?"

"Enjoying the assembly!" Louisa retorted, wrenching her arm free and glaring at her sister. "Why the need for a search party?"

"We were worried about you!" Juliet said, tugging at a crease in her skirts with vehemence.

"You needn't have been!" Louisa smiled. "Good evening, Auntie! What a wonderful night this has been. Edmund, why don't you take Juliet for one more dance? She needs to burn off some of her energy and not direct it into worrying over people who do not need her concern." She lifted her head and smiled, looking lighter and more like her old self than Edmund had seen her since their party's arrival in London. "I am perfectly well."

Chapter Twelve

A day or two after the assembly, Julie was pleased to finally secure some quiet time to herself, to think and to write.

She had been floating since that evening when the tide had finally seemed to turn and Mrs Gale at last softened towards her. There had been no apology, but then Juliet had not expected one. There had been no true acknowledgement, either, of the unkindness she had subjected her soon-to-be daughter-in-law to, or the fact that it had been her intervention that had first separated the pair. Juliet was simply grateful to have an end to hostilities, though, and it had been a peculiar blessing to hear Mrs Gale praise her character and - more unbelievable, still! - her writing to a group of her most elegant friends.

If word is to circulate that I am an author, I had better have something to show for my time! she thought, as, with a stern frown, she rearranged her writing implements on the small writing desk before her. She smoothed out a scrap of paper, but when inspiration did not immediately strike her, returned to the last pieces she had written, re-reading them with a critical eye and trying to sink back into the world her pen had created.

Has the clock always ticked so loudly? She cast a critical eye to the mantel before returning to her work, massaging her temples and willing herself to concentrate.

A muffled conversation at the door to the small library distracted her next, and she strained to hear, discerning her father and mother were recalling that she had asked not to be disturbed and thus they would retreat to the parlour and not bother her. With a groan, she sank forward on her desk, abandoning all attempts to write anything at all. Why was it that her mind could be tumbling with ideas one moment, usually when she was expressly unable to write a word, but when she carved out time specifically for the task, she could conjure nothing at all?

Shuffling her papers together, she returned the whole to her writing case and stood, stalking towards the door and throwing it open, calling after her parents to wait.

"Mama, Papa! I will join you." She sighed, smiling ruefully. "I do not think I shall manage to write any more today."

"Oh, dear!" Mrs Turner tutted, sliding her arm around her daughter and walking as one down the narrow corridor. "I do hope we did not disturb you?"

"No," Juliet shrugged her thin shoulders. "I haven't been able to concentrate all morning."

"Too many exciting things rumbling around that head of yours!" Mrs Turner beamed, and Mr Turner, behind them, harrumphed as if he did not agree with this assessment nor entirely approve of it.

"Something like that," Juliet confessed, unable to keep the smile from creeping onto her cheeks. She and her mother had taken the time the previous day, while the rest of the house slept off the effects of the assembly, to peruse the shops and she, at last, was making some progress towards having her trousseau completed. This was another concern lifted, for she did not like shopping the way Louisa did. Her sister had lent her talents the previous day, too, and seemed so much like her old self that any lingering concerns Juliet had felt towards Louisa on account of Mr Weston had also been somewhat alleviated. She still disliked the man and longed far more than was ladylike to sock him squarely in the jaw for the pain he had caused her flighty sister, but if Louisa did not seem to bear a grudge then it seemed entirely unnecessary for Juliet to.

Perhaps it was never as serious as I gave it credit, she had told herself, recalling that Louisa seemed entirely capable of falling in love at the drop of a handkerchief, with any and every eligible, handsome young man she spied.

"Where is Louisa?" she asked, now feeling as if she would rather like to include her sister in this familial hour, for their aunt and uncle were out visiting friends and had given the Turners the run of the house in their absence. As much as she loved her aunt and uncle, Juliet could not help but be selfish for her closest family members, conscious that, once married, their relationships would alter in a hundred small but significant ways.

"Asleep," Mr Turner said, sitting down and attending to his pipe, the use of which had been banned by his sister, but which he would quite contentedly smoke in her absence. "I have not yet seen her today." His eyes twinkled with merriment, for Louisa's habit of sleeping late was a source of perpetual teasing from her family when at home. Juliet had thought the excitement of being in London would put a stop to it, but by now the thrill of being in town had worn off and Louisa's old habits had resurfaced.

"We shall have you all to ourselves!" Mrs Turner remarked, reluctantly letting go of her hold on her daughter so that the ladies might sit and await the arrival of the tea things.

Juliet smiled, unsurprised to see a glimmer of sadness in her mother's usually merry face.

"You act as if you are losing me, Mama! You know, even when I am married, that Edmund and I shall run over to Aston House just as often as he does now!" She laughed. "You shall never truly be rid of me!"

Mrs Turner smiled, quite content with this suggestion.

"I think it likely we may even see more of Mrs Gale, too, as she has at last seen fit to lower her defences and accept me as her son's choice." Juliet drew in a heavy breath, relishing the absence of the crushing weight on her shoulders that had been her mother-in-law's opposition.

"As well she ought!" Mr Turner remarked from his corner, clenching his teeth around the stem of his pipe.

"Now, dear! You know that family is not always so agreeable as that. It can be difficult for us to loosen our grip on those we love."

Mrs Turner's tone of voice was sanguine enough, but Juliet did not miss the significance of her words. Her mother understood, only too well, what it was to be at the mercy of one's husband's family. Aunt Brierley had never quite forgiven her brother for marrying the way he had chosen, although she had never openly criticised Mrs Turner the two women had never been close. Juliet slipped a hand around her mother's and squeezed in silent encouragement.

"Well, we need not fret. At least now Mrs Gale seems to have resolved whatever concern she had about the marriage.

The two of you looked quite comfortable together last evening -"

Before Juliet could reply or anybody say more, the door opened to announce a guest, and Mr and Mrs Turner looked at each other with surprise as Mrs Gale herself was ushered into the cramped parlour.

"Good day!" she declared, as the group greeted one another. "I hope you do not mind my arriving unannounced." She turned to Juliet, a tentative smile on her face. "My son has absented himself for the day to go to his club." She grimaced, as if the notion of spending a day in the club was more than she could countenance. "I wonder, then, if you might be willing to join me on a walk, Juliet? I know you are fond of it, and I am aching for some exercise."

This was perhaps the most honest and direct Juliet had ever known Mrs Gale to be, and she was so stunned she could think of nothing to say other than to agree. Desperately she glanced towards her mother, whose attention was on her teacup, offering no help. Juliet wavered. Whilst she and Mrs Gale had made progress at the assembly, she was not sure they would yet manage an hour's conversation on a walk, without some assistance.

"Perhaps my sister might care to join us, Mrs Gale, if you do not mind my inviting her?"

"Oh, by all means!" Mrs Gale sat, gratefully receiving the cup of tea she was offered. "I shall take tea with your parents for a moment or two while you ask her, and then we shall depart."

Relieved, Juliet fled, taking the stairs two at a time and barely pausing to knock at Louisa's door before flinging it open.

"Lou, come out with me, won't you?"

She had uttered the question without looking and stopped short, surprised to find her sister's room empty, the bed neatly made and the window left open for air. Juliet frowned. Louisa was not asleep, then, as Papa had presumed. She must have gone out very early. Juliet's frown lessened. No, perhaps not. She had been closeted away at her work, abiding no distractions. Of course Louisa would merely have gone about her tasks without knocking or alerting her to her departure.

Well, I am happy for her, Juliet thought. It was an encouraging sign that Louisa had found friends enough to go out with, and she would not begrudge her that, even though it now left Juliet with no alternative but to spend an hour with her soon-to-be mother-in-law entirely alone. Drawing a fortifying breath, she forced a smile onto her face and retraced her steps towards the parlour, determined to make the afternoon a success, even without Louisa's assistance.

EDMUND WANDERED THROUGH the streets of London, nodding greetings at acquaintances as he passed them but with no real destination in mind.

He had gone out early, planning to call on Nash at his aunt's house. His friend had not been at home, however, and it had cost Edmund a quarter-hour of polite conversation with Nash's aunt before he could extract himself from her clutches and embrace his freedom once more.

He was not entirely sure his vague wandering was truly *embracing* anything. With a sigh he consulted his watch and altered his course, walking with purpose towards his club. The club was the excuse he had given Mama, after all. Better to make it true by at least showing his face. It had been a while since he was last here, and he wondered, idly, who he might.

Comfortably ensconced in a chair with a drink to nurse and any one of a dozen newspapers to read, Edmund felt the same rest that found him only in places like this. It was not home, but it was comfortable, the gentle sort of society with his peers and friends the kind that required little effort on his part.

This afternoon the place was quiet, peppered with only a few older gentlemen avoiding their wives and talking business. He glanced towards the billiard table, seeing it occupied and looked back to his newspaper, feeling a strange pang of isolation. Edmund was not prone to loneliness, being agreeable and finding friends wherever he went, but this morning all those friends appeared otherwise engaged. *I shall enjoy time alone, in that case,* he told himself, trying desperately to engage his faculties with the opinion of the editor on matters in the Peninsula, and only serving to grow drowsy. He shot an angry look towards the hearth, where an unseasonably warm fire blazed and decided the heat was to blame for his lack of energy. Scooping up his drink and setting aside his newspaper he strolled towards the billiards table, exchanging pleasantries with the small group of gentlemen he saw hunched over there.

"Gale!"

Erasmus Finch, his old friend, barrelled past the crowd to embrace him, shaking his hand so thoroughly that Edmund felt his whole body jogged out of his stupor.

"What are you doing here?" Finch's eyes gleamed with interest, sensing a story. "I thought you were content always to remain in the countryside, demanding your friends come to see *you* when you could not be bothered to see them?"

"You enjoyed my hospitality well enough," Edmund retorted, taking a sip of his drink and recalling, with a grimace, the events that had conspired to encourage him to invite Erasmus, with others, to stay at Northridge to begin with. Had he ever truly entertained the idea of matching Madeline Turner with this man? He shook his head, dispelling the notion. No, Maddy had made her own choice and a far better one than either he or Juliet might have managed.

He smiled a little, recalling the bet they had made, and how it had been an attempt, on his part, simply to turn Juliet's mind to marriage, thinking, logically enough, that once she had matched her sister she would turn to her own future happiness. It had not happened quite like that, but still, he dared to think that the year would not be progressing as it was now, had they not made that first winter wager.

"Aye, the country is all well and good for a visit, but for *life?*" Erasmus boomed, opening his arms wide as if to encapsulate the entirety of the club. "But come, you did not come here to debate modes of living, I am quite sure. What brings you to London, and what brings you here?" His eyebrows lifted as if on the scent of scandal. "I hear tell you are to be married, Gale. Tell me you are not tiring already of your wife before she is even legally that?"

The idea that Edmund would trade time with Juliet for the smoky, stuffy interior of his club struck him as amusing and he swallowed a laugh, disguising it unsuccessfully as a cough.

"No, I do not tire of her," he said, taking a sip of his drink. "But nor do I feel a compulsion to be forever by her side." He gave Erasmus a shrewd look. "You know both Juliet and I value our freedom too much to hamper it in one another."

"Juliet." Erasmus stroked the reedy beginnings of a beard. "I suppose I oughtn't to be surprised you should marry her, for the two of you were a dreadful pair when we were all together at Christmas. Still, I can't help but marvel you did not wait for the youngest sister. She was by far the prettiest."

Erasmus made a rolling grunt of laughter and Edmund felt entirely irritated by the suggestion that any young lady would be preferable to him than Juliet. He could not even distinguish his friend's words as complimentary to Louisa, who he had grown still more protective of since Nash's folly. The reminder of Louisa recalled the purpose of Edmund's errand to him, and he straightened, downing the last of his drink and setting the glass down on a nearby table.

"I don't suppose you have seen Weston anywhere, have you?" He raked a hand through his dark hair, adjusting his collars and cuffs. "I have been halfway around London looking for the fellow this morning and turned up nothing."

Erasmus made an expansive shrug.

"Your guess is as good as mine. He remained at Northridge long after I left, recall." He glanced at Edmund out of the corner of his shifty eyes. "Why are you so desperate to find him? Does he owe you money too?"

Edmund frowned, surprised to hear the bitterness in his old friend's voice.

"Money? No. Then has he -"

"He did me out of my winnings on more than one occasion," Erasmus grumbled, as if the notion of losing money was almost more objectionable than the fact that he had lost it to someone claiming to be a friend. "I had heard he was back in

London and thought at last that he would seek to make good on his debts but the fellow is doing his best to avoid me."

"He has a lot on his mind," Edmund murmured, recalling the surprise he felt to hear of Nash's engagement and the explanation that Weston's aunt had been only too keen to labour that morning. *My poor nephew has shirked his duties for too long but at last he has tired of running around the country with a gaggle of reprobate gentlemen. He seeks to settle into the marriage I ordained for him more years ago than I care to admit!* This marriage was not Nash's choice, then, for which Edmund could afford some sympathy, although that did not excuse his caddish behaviour around Louisa.

If only I could find the man, I might learn the truth of the matter myself! he thought, adding a mental note to warn him that Erasmus was on the warpath and wished to have his money back, one way or another.

"Well, let us not speak of our troubles, Gale," Erasmus said, his mood lifting with the prospect of a drink with an old friend. "Come, you'll have another brandy? And perhaps we shall give that chess set some exercise. I seem to recall our last match ended in a draw. Let us see if one or other of us can be the victor on this occasion..."

Chapter Thirteen

It had seemed like wisdom to suggest they met in one of London's many parks, and Nash knew he ought to be grateful for the relative anonymity provided him by the crowd. Instead, he saw only more and more potential witnesses.

They are not looking at me, he told himself. *They do not even notice me!*

This was not entirely true, for he had caught the eye of several young ladies out walking with their beaux or mamas. He affixed a bland smile to his face and turned away, focusing on the pond and pretending to watch the ducks that swam across it.

In truth, he saw nothing at all, his mind already condemning him for such a reckless action as the one he had suggested to Louisa Turner. Running away from his own unwanted future was one thing. He would burn bridges with his aunt and cousin, but bridges could be mended in time and he put enough faith in his ability to charm that he thought it entirely likely he might win over his aunt at least a little. The whole of his inheritance would be gone, but she would no doubt soften and indulge him in a gift or two. But for Louisa, running away with a gentleman was to court scandal.

It, too, would be forgiven. Once they were married, he had no doubt, they would be welcomed back if not quite with open arms then at least with tolerance and acceptance. He had to hope they would be, for Mr Turner was his last, best hope of securing any kind of fortune. It would not be much, for the Turners were not wealthy, but neither were they impoverished. Louisa's sisters, too, had successfully secured wealthy matches that he felt at least a little certain of some care from those quarters. They would not wish to see their sister starve, at least.

He kicked at a spot of gravel, loathing the turn his thoughts had taken. It was too cruel, to be placed in the position of begging simply because one wished to marry the young lady one chose, and not the one others chose for you. He would rather be penniless with Louisa Turner by his side than wealthy without her, wouldn't he? He thought so. No, he knew so.

Confident, then, that he was making the right decision, the only decision he could make in his position, he straightened, turning just as a certain young lady came hurrying towards him, glancing furtively around in a manner that did not serve to render her invisible, as she thought. Swallowing a curse, he strode forward, greeting Louisa and quickly drawing her to his side.

"I have done it!" she giggled triumphantly. "Nobody even saw me leave. It will be hours before they miss me and think to search." Her eyes sparkled with fun at what she thought of as a great adventure. Nash wished he could match her enthusiasm. He stopped walking, forcing her to look at him carefully and spoke with an urgency that scared even him.

"Are you sure you want to do this, Louisa? There will be no easy retreat once we make our move."

"Of course I am sure!" Louisa laughed, before the sight of Nash's face made her smile fall. "Have you changed your mind?"

Nash shook his head, drawing his lips into a tight smile. He hadn't. Now that she was here, he was even more convicted of his course. He loved her, truly, he did, and he could not fathom a future where they would not be together. If courting scandal was the only way to ensure that, then let them court it. Hang society and its expectations. *Hang Aunt Reed and her wealth! I will not allow her to use it to control me any longer!*

"Then why do you look so serious?" Louisa teased him, her smile growing. "We are embarking upon an adventure, Nash. The kind of romantic escape Julie could only dream of." There was a hint of superiority in her smile. "How shocked she will be when she hears! How shocked all my sisters will be to realise, all along, that despite their claims to romance mine was one truly lifted from the pages of a novel!"

Nash paused, wondering fleetingly if it was the promise of life with him or an adventure to rival that of each of her sisters combined, truly underpinned Louisa's desire to flee London. He did not give the thought a moment to take root, though. They were here and they were together and that was all that mattered.

"Have you made arrangements?" Louisa asked, as they continued to circle the path, conversing in whispers indistinguishable from a dozen other young courting couples.

"I have secured us passage by stage," Nash assured her. "We must join it in a few minutes, and it will take us north."

"To Scotland?" Louisa breathed, her excitement palpable.

"Eventually." Nash smiled, grimly, wondering if Louisa had any notion of the distance of the journey they were to embark upon. "We shall have to stop a time or two on the way."

Louisa's expression fell and she struggled to conceal her surprise.

"It is quite some distance to Scotland."

"But - surely people will catch up to us." Louisa bit her lip. "My parents may not notice I am gone immediately, but they will notice. What is to say they will not come after us, or even overtake us on the road?"

Nash sighed, patiently.

"There is no guarantee of anything." He shrugged, brusquely. "But if they discover us together it will not be too difficult to persuade them to consent to the marriage."

Louisa frowned, a little surprised by this shift in his usually easy-going attitude.

"I am quite sure my father would have consented if you had proposed in the usual way," she said, meekly. "I am not the one who is not free -"

"This is our only option," Nash insisted, holding Louisa's arm so tightly that she yelped and he relinquished his hold with a muttered apology.

"Come, let us take one more turn about the park before we go to meet the carriage. Our journey will be long, so we must make the most of fresh air and activity while it is afforded us."

This was the very best thing he might have said, for it allowed Louisa the chance to think of the future and chatter happily about all that lay ahead of them. Their flight and hasty marriage at Gretna Green - if they made it so far - was an obstacle. Far better to think beyond it, of the home they would build together, of their future happiness.

Her voice was a balm to Nash's soul, soothing his fractured nerves. Yes, this was the right course of action. It was risky, but what was not in these days? Without risk, there would be no reward, and he held his reward beside him. *Let Aunt do as she will. I will marry as I choose and be happy!*

LOUISA HAD NEVER BEEN fond of travelling. Whilst she enjoyed the promise of being elsewhere, home being so familiar and dull to her when contrasted with the thrilling prospect of London or Bath, she rarely enjoyed the physical ordeal of travelling by coach.

Today, though, she barely noticed any discomfort, so enraptured was she by the adventure she and Nash were embarking upon. She shoved aside any anxieties and scrunched her eyes closed, determined to seal every moment in her memory. This was her grand adventure, the tale she would tell over and over to her children, of how their mother had been brave and impetuous and in love.

"Can you move over a little?"

Louisa's eyes flew open and she looked at Nash, surprised he had addressed her not in a warm, love-filled voice but one that was as matter-of-fact as if they were strangers. He gestured to the space on her side of the bench and she obliged, pressing herself tightly into one corner and allowing him a little more space to sit comfortably.

"Much obliged."

She opened her mouth to say something else, caught between affection and a cynical retort, but before she could form a word he had turned abruptly away from her and engaged the older gentleman on his other side in a worldly discussion of business and the profit margins one was afforded in the silk trade.

Louisa turned away, fixing her eyes on the countryside that rumbled past their window and tried not to cry. She swallowed past a painful lump in her throat before coming once more to her senses. Giving herself a shake, she rearranged her features into a smile, knowing that nobody could ever admire a young lady who pouted.

This leg of our journey could never truly be called romantic, she reminded herself. *We are on the stage with strangers! And Nash must keep up the pretence of our travelling together as if we have done it often. Too much affection or overbearing concern for my wellbeing would betray us immediately.*

She nodded to herself, her confidence growing in this explanation the longer she considered it. Yes, this was much the better way. Nash might make polite conversation with his neighbour and she, too, would seek to befriend hers. That was what travellers did, was it not? She cleared her throat, looking across the faces of the three folks sitting opposite them, and eventually settled on the youngest of the three, a pale, grey-featured young lady who attended to some piecework, stitching quite miraculously quickly and neatly and succeeding in not only keeping her seams straight but never once pricking her nimble fingers. Louisa was quite taken with this display of genius, until the young lady glanced up, her gaze meeting Louisa's with suspicion.

"Oh!" Louisa squeaked, forcing a smile onto her face that she hoped would charm this stranger as easily as it had done numerous handsome young men. The young lady's gaze hardened, and Louisa dropped the smile as quickly as she had assumed it, casting about for some word she might offer in its place.

"I admire your - your bonnet. It is very...pretty..." she trailed off, lamely. This was a lie, for the bonnet was not only old, it was ugly, and surely originally designed for someone other than its current wearer. Nonetheless, the young lady reached up to pat it, as if she wore a literal crown, smiling condescendingly at Louisa but saying nothing, and returning with fervour to her stitching.

Louisa sighed, looking back towards the window. Her first attempt to engage a fellow traveller in a conversation had not gone well, and Nash was ignoring her in favour of a lively discussion of overseas markets. She shifted uncomfortably, rubbing the elbow that had been wedged against the hard wooden door of their carriage.

Perhaps this was not such a marvellous idea, she thought, feeling very sorry for herself and conjuring an image of her family at home in Aunt Brierley's house. They would be sitting around the parlour talking or playing games. Juliet would be scribbling away at her infernal novel, or holding court as she spoke of her wedding plans and the purchases for her trousseau that she had been making...

Louisa frowned, her resolve hardening.

This is my chance for romance. I could not sit around at home and wait for it to find me. How likely would it be that a third eligible suitor should find his way to Aston House? She recalled, with something that might have been jealousy, how quickly and easily both Maddy and Bess had been singled out and chosen by newcomers to Castleford. She should not have wished to court attention from either Mr Hodge or Mr Cluett, although she supposed they made fine enough companions for her sisters.

Still, their beaux could not possibly have loved them as much as Nash loves me. He has given up his inheritance, gone against the hopes of his family - for me! Her expression lifted as she felt warmth flood her body at the remembrance of their covert meeting at the assembly. He had told her then, in no uncertain terms, that he loved her, that he wanted to be with her, and that he was willing to cast everything else aside to allow that to happen.

It is only right that I suffer a little too, she thought, ignoring the ache in her hip and pressing herself still more closely into the corner so that Nash might have more space with which to gesticulate in his animated conversation. She would endure the most uncomfortable carriage journey imaginable if it meant she might be Mrs Nash Weston.

For this is what true love is! she marvelled. *My story is the most romantic of them all, and I am living it, right now!*

Chapter Fourteen

"Are you sure I cannot persuade you to join us for tea, Mrs Gale?"

"No, no! I have taken up too much of your time already!" Edmund's mother patted Juliet's arm warmly as the two ladies parted company a little way from Aunt Brierley's house. "I hope I shall see you again soon, though, my dear. Do call on us at home, won't you? I don't know why Edmund is so reluctant to have people..." An idea seemed to occur to her all at once and she called after Juliet. "In fact, we must host a dinner. I shall write to invite you!"

Juliet smiled, waving and almost skipping the last few steps towards home. She could not believe that she had spent an enjoyable afternoon with Mrs Gale. So enjoyable that she was almost a little disappointed that she could not persuade the older lady to join them for refreshments. She smiled as she let herself into the house, humming as she removed her bonnet. How quickly things could change!

There was a noticeable hum in the air as she made her way down the corridor towards the parlour, and Juliet could see servants hurrying this way and that, muttering between themselves and all eagerly averting their gaze from hers. It was on the tip of her tongue to enquire what was the matter when her aunt's voice reached her ears.

"What do you mean, gone? Please, dear, speak plainly. You have always possessed a habit of obfuscating the truth, it is most unbecoming -"

"I have told you all I know," Mrs Turner replied, her voice trembling with anxiety and annoyance. "If you do not credit my explanations, perhaps you had better go out in search of your brother, although I assure you he knows no more than I do!"

Juliet opened the door to the parlour as her mother collapsed into a chair, fanning herself with agitation.

"Is something the matter?"

"Oh, Juliet! For a moment I thought you were Louisa and all this might have come to nothing."

Juliet cast a glance at her mother, whose face was pale and drawn, lines etched deep with worry. She could almost not believe the change wrought over her mother in the space of a few hours.

"Mama? What has happened?" She crossed the parlour quickly and perched on the chair nearest her mother, reaching for her hand and bidding her meet her gaze.

"Well you may ask -" Aunt Brierley began, growing ostentatious in her concern.

"Louisa is missing." Mrs Turner spoke simply, quietly, but directly to the point, undercutting Mrs Brierley's great revelation and provoking her to sniff irritably and fold her arms, giving vent to her frustrations in tapping her foot.

"Missing?" Juliet frowned. "But she cannot be missing, surely?" She looked at her aunt then back to her mother, seeing nothing but a confirmation of this as truth in the faces of both ladies.

"I know she was not at home when I went out this afternoon, but I thought it likely she had found friends and gone out to socialise. Are you sure -"

"She has no such group of friends that we can think of," Mrs Turner said, biting her lip until it turned white. "None of the servants knew where she had gone, and she would have told us. She would have told someone, surely!"

Juliet nodded, discerning the truth of the matter quicker than her mother and not daring to speak of it. If Louisa had escaped the house without notice, it was because she had chosen to. She was not given to quietly creeping around unless she was up to something.

"I shall go and look for her," she began, leaping to her feet. "Do not worry Mama, Auntie. I am sure I shall -"

"Your father and uncle have gone already," Mrs Turner said, trying to smile and not quite succeeding. "And your aunt and I were just debating where else we might send servants."

"You do not know where your foolish young sister might have run away to, do you?" Aunt Brierley asked. "Or with whom?"

Juliet shook her head, trying to recall if she had noticed Louisa favour anybody in particular at the assembly. It had been the only social occasion both sisters had attended and was the only real chance Louisa had had to make new acquaintances or renew old ones...

Juliet's breath caught in her throat, and her mother whirled to look at her.

"What do you know?" She grasped tight hold of Juliet's fore-arm and dug her fingers in, scarcely aware of the pain she was causing. "Juliet, what are you thinking?"

"I am mistaken, surely," Juliet said, working her arm free and clenching and unclenching her hand into a fist. "It was a fleeting thought, an unlikely one at that, but..."

"Speak, do, and let go of all these deadly qualifiers!" Aunt Brierley cried, throwing her hands up in despair. Ordinarily, Juliet might have taken her reaction personally, believing herself to bear the brunt of her aunt's anger, but she could see, from the pinched and drawn expression on her aunt's face that it was worry, not anger, that made her reactions so extreme.

"The only person I can think of Louisa knowing well enough to meet - and whom she would not be eager to meet *here*, amongst the rest of us - is Mr Weston." Her eyes met her mother's widening in concern. "But she would not...you do not think..."

"I am inclined to believe Mr Weston capable of almost anything at all!" Mrs Turner got to her feet, hurrying over to a writing desk and scratching out a note. She summoned a servant and passed them the missive, instructing them to find Mr Turner or Colonel Brierley and deliver it, then return with an update on their progress.

Her task accomplished, she sagged back, reaching out to steady herself against the wall. Juliet leapt up to support her mother but another lady was closer, and Mrs Brierley put a strong arm around her sister-in-law, rocking her as gently and tenderly as if she were a child.

"Come, now, dear. Don't let's despair. You know how sensible your daughters are...for more than my own ever were. I have always thought you were a much better mother than I, and you shall reap the benefit of that now..."

Juliet crept backwards, sinking into her seat and watching the two women come together in a way she had once thought impossible, and prayed that her aunt was right.

BY THE TIME EDMUND extracted himself from the grasp of his friends - for Erasmus had not been the only familiar face begging to be reacquainted with the long-absent, much-missed Mr Gale - he was surprised to feel his spirits lifting. He had missed his friends more than he had realised, and would remember that in future.

He whistled as he made his way slowly home, pleased with his use of the day, even if he had not succeeded in finding Nash and having the difficult conversation he knew he must. No matter, he would cheerfully leave that challenge for another day.

He rounded a corner and came quite suddenly to a stop as he spotted two familiar gentlemen up ahead, stopping people as they passed with increasing urgency and asking each a question that was met with sympathetic shrugs and shaking heads.

His good mood evaporated almost immediately and Edmund forsook his stroll to jog down the street, reaching Mr Turner and Colonel Brierley in a moment.

"Good afternoon! Is there a problem?"

"A problem? Yes, you may well say - oh, Mr Gale. Excellent, yes." Mr Turner was looking rumpled, and he removed his hat to rake his hand through his hair, worsening its appearance considerably before turning back to the milling crowd that was drawing around them. "Have you seen a young lady, by any chance?"

Edmund grasped Mr Turner's arm, firmly but not unkindly, and forced the man to look at him.

"What has happened?"

"Why, it is Louisa." Mr Turner blinked as if he could not quite believe the words to be true, even as he uttered them.

"What about her?"

"She is gone."

Edmund frowned, shaking his head as he tried to make sense of his friend's words.

"Gone? Gone where?"

"Gone." Mr Turner shrugged his shoulders, blinking rapidly as if he, too, was struggling to process this information. "Vanished. Disappeared. We cannot find her anywhere."

Edmund could sense the growing interest of a crowd and, fearing to provoke gossip and put both Louisa and her family at the centre of a scandal that might not exist, he took the arms of both gentlemen and steered them across the threshold of the nearest inn. Securing them a quiet table, he ordered a healthy measure of brandy for each of them and waited until they had drunk to ask the question again.

"Tell me from the beginning," he said, addressing his question to Mr Turner, whilst keeping a keen eye on the man's brother-in-law, who seemed to be handling the disaster with far less grace than Mr Turner.

"We did not realise she was not at home," Mr Turner confessed, taking out his handkerchief and wiping his forehead. "We thought she merely kept to her room, sleeping late. You know how Louisa can be..."

Edmund nodded, recalling many a time he had called at Aston House only to find her slowly emerging from slumber at some surprisingly late hour.

"Juliet went to invite her out - she spent the afternoon with your mother, you see. I suppose she might be home now, and she will have to be told. Oh dear..."

"Mr Turner," Edward said, sharply but not unkindly.

"Ah, yes." The older man swallowed. "Well, in any case, Juliet went to her room and found it empty. We all assumed that Louisa was out with friends, you see, she is such a gregarious, outgoing young lady - well, you know. She makes friends everywhere she goes!"

Edmund nodded, although he did not quite have as much faith in Louisa's ability to make only friends wherever she went. He had witnessed enough of her feuds over the years to think it entirely possible she made enemies with equal ease, but now was not the time for that. *And in any case, a falling out over a hair-ribbon is hardly cause for a disappearance!*

"Have you managed to track down her friends and ask them?" he asked, making a mental list of names so that he might aid the two elder gentlemen in their task.

"Well, that is the dilemma!" Mr Turner confessed. "We know of none." He seemed to recognise Edmund before him for the first time and leaned forward, grasping tightly to his arm. "Do you know? You and Juliet, surely you know other young people in London, those that might know Louisa, places she might like to go to?"

Edmund smiled, wishing to be reassuring but all the while unnerved by this question. He did not have the first idea who Louisa was friends with in London, and all of the places that he was fond of frequenting he could not imagine housing his dainty little friend. His heart sank. There was one person Louisa knew in London, and who would have any number of places in mind where they might spend their time, away from the care of her family and the interference of his.

"I have an idea - not where to find her, but an idea of someone who might have seen her." He glanced at his watch, trying to calculate how long Louisa had been missing from the vague account he had received from her uncle and father. His heart grew stony. Nash would not be so foolish, surely, as to elope?

He is engaged to another, he reminded himself, but even that excuse felt hollow when he recalled his meeting with Nash's aunt and cousin that day. The engagement was surely not a happy one, nor any circumstance Nash rejoiced in.

Let us imagine he might be desperate enough to consider it, then, surely we can give Louisa more credit than that. She is no fool. She would not allow herself to be swept away by the impetuous, foolish actions of a gentleman who is not free to offer for her.

This thought comforted him for all of half a moment. He recalled the lovesick look Louisa had worn at the assembly when he caught sight of her and Nash, and his heart sank still further. Yes, he could just see how the matter might play out. Louisa, affronted at being the only one of her sisters not engaged or married would be eager for any sort of admiration. And Nash was adept at getting what he wanted. Was Edmund himself not a testament to that, having housed his friend at cost for the past several months?

He will not throw away his chance at an estate, he told himself. *Not for as modest a dowry as Louisa Turner might offer.*

Yet, had not people done more foolish things throughout history on account of love? If Nash's affections for Louisa were genuine, and Edmund had to believe they were, might he justify any action he chose to take as the actions of a man in love? Nash was flighty and idiotic, charming to a fault, but he was not cruel. He did not make a habit of encouraging ladies he had no feeling for.

I only hope his feelings for Louisa are genuine, he thought, grimly. *For if my fears are correct and they have run away together, he shall have no way out of this mess but to marry her!*

Chapter Fifteen

By the time they tripped over the threshold of the small inn partway along their journey, Louisa was exhausted. Her limbs and joints ached from the combination of being cramped into the corner of a carriage and jostled with every turn of the wheel, for whilst they had broken their journey, their travel was far less comfortable than that which she was used to.

Nash did not seem to mind it, for he chattered with his fellow travellers and moved as if he was used to such discomforts and found them amusing, rather than painful.

"M'dear," he said, turning and passing her the key to the room she had insisted on taking, separate from his. That he had even hesitated when the innkeeper enquired after their requirements made her blush scarlet, even now, although he had, at length, declared they would require two rooms.

"Aren't we to dine?" Louisa asked, casting an anxious glance into the dining area, which was dominated with loud, male voices, with only one or two spare tables open to them. A whiff of stew caught Louisa's nostrils and her stomach growled with hunger.

"I thought you would prefer to take a tray to your room, Lou," Nash remarked, his attention already captured by a tense card game that was taking place in one corner of the room. "Surely this is no place for a lady." He winked as he said it and

Louisa snatched the key from him, stalking upstairs without a backwards glance. Where was the doting Nash Weston she thought she knew? The man who would lay his coat over a puddle to save her shoes when they walked?

I wonder if he ever existed at all, she thought, miserably. Reaching the numbered room that was to be hers, she placed the key in the lock, jiggling it and reinserting it several times until at last the lock caught and turned, and the door swung open on creaking hinges. The little room was clean but sparse, yet Louisa did not seem to notice. In a stupor, she stumbled across the bare wooden floor and flopped face-first onto the bed, ignoring the vaguely musty smell of the worn cotton bedspread.

What have I done? She curled up on the bed, not even bothering to remove her shoes. Hot tears coursed down her cheeks and she drew in a ragged, shaky breath. She hugged her knees into her chest and thought over all that had happened today. She might have imagined some hardships on their road to romance, but she had never imagined this! Holed up - alone! - in an anonymous inn, with no word of what would happen next. She had barely succeeded in drawing Nash to speak of his plans for the next leg of their journey, only that it would continue tomorrow, at first light.

There was a light knock at the door and for one wild, fleeting moment, Louisa thought it might be Nash, coming to apologise and to escort her down to dinner. Maybe he had had a word with the innkeeper and arranged for them to have a table in the back, somewhere quiet. There would be a clean white table-cloth and candles, and their dinner would be brought to them on silver platters, and they would eat and talk and smile...

"One moment!" she called, hurrying to her feet. There was a small wash-stand with dusty-looking water but she poured some into the bowl, all the same, splashing her face and washing her hands. She raked damp fingers through her hair, plastering down those curls which had come loose with the exertion of travelling and began to feel the tiniest bit more human again. It was not the same as if she had had her own home-comforts on hand, but it was better than she had looked and felt even a few moments earlier. Tripping lightly to the door, she pulled it open, smiling and agreeing to Nash's suggestion before it was even made.

"Dinner, Miss?"

Her smile fell. It was not Nash that stood before her but an old, weary-looking servant, who held out a tray of tea, jam and bread. Louisa did not reach out for it right away and the woman shrugged, causing the tea things to rattle.

"The gentleman said you were tired and wished to take a small supper in your room." She held the tray out and dumbly Louisa took it, standing open-mouthed as she watched the woman slope off.

There would be no elegant dinner with Nash, then. No candlelight, no linens.

For a moment Louisa had the fleeting urge to jettison the entire tray, to launch it at the floor and relish the sound of crashing plates and broken crockery. She resisted, though, setting it down on a low table that must serve as dresser, end-table, writing desk and all. She was very hungry and eyed the thick slice of fresh bread with eagerness. Her hands shook as she poured her tea, and spread thick, homemade strawberry jam on the bread, cramming half a slice into her mouth in one go.

I am just weary from travel, she told herself, already feeling her spirits lift a little with the first few bites of food. *I will eat and sleep and tomorrow I will feel better again. This is what I wanted, after all.* She swallowed, reaching for her tea and washing the bread and jam down with one scalding sip. *This is exactly what I wanted.*

THIS IS NOT WHAT I wanted, Nash thought, as he nursed a watered-down beer and watched two burly-looking men proceed to arm-wrestle, as a group of their friends noisily cheered one or other of them on, wagering extravagantly on the outcome.

The last look Louisa had given him had been piteous, filled with reproach, and it was that he saw whenever he closed his eyes. That, and his aunt. He could just imagine her thrashing about the house, calling him every name under the sun and trying to orchestrate some way to manage the social fall-out from his flight. She would cut him off completely, or she would construct some other story to save face, but either way, he would not escape without feeling the full force of her wrath. He shuddered, lifting his glass and draining it in a long, bitter swig. He waved it to the innkeeper, who took it from him and refilled it, returning it to him with a vague nod.

There was nothing to be gained from lingering here. He had no money to speak of, or not enough to waste on gambling, even if he could be certain of a return. He eyed his fellow drinkers warily, thinking that these would not be so gentlemanly about debts as his friends might have been.

His heart sank. He had not thought about how this would affect his friends. The story would spread like wildfire. How could it not? Edmund owed him nothing, and when he discovered that Nash had not only fled his obligations but persuaded Louisa Turner to come with him, there would be no mercy. His hand shook as he lifted his glass. They would notice she was gone now. The family would be frantic, tearing about London looking for her. Not for the effect their disappearance would have on *his* family did he lament, but for the Turners. They had been nothing but kind to him, welcoming him as one of their own friends. He thought of kind-hearted Mr Turner, so like the father he might have wanted in place of his own. Of Mrs Turner, who was everything his self-interested, proud aunt was not. Of the sisters, all of whom would be his now, too, once he and Louisa were married. Would it be enough, he wondered, the fact of their marriage, to overcome the scandal of how it had come about? *It will have to be*, Nash counselled himself. *There is no turning back now.*

The door to the inn banged open and on reflex, Nash glanced towards it, never once expecting to recognise the late arrival. When he did, his blood ran cold in his veins and it was pure luck that he managed to keep hold of his cup, setting it shakily down on the table next to him and backing away as Edmund Gale strode into the inn.

"Excuse me," he called to the innkeeper. "Is there a man here by the name of Gale?"

He was breathless with the exertion of riding, for his clothes suggested he had come without a carriage. It would be quicker, Nash supposed, if his goal had been pursuit. He was not quick enough to conceal himself, or perhaps he did not truly wish to. Here was the escape he had longed for, however much he dreaded it.

"I am here," he murmured, stepping forward and greeting Edmund with a wary smile. "Well travelled, Ed. You have discovered us."

The tiniest shadow flickered across Edmund's face at that single word, *us*. In it, his worst fears were confirmed, and he looked as if he could quite contentedly lash out at his friend.

"Where is Louisa?" he asked, pulling off his gloves and dropping them next to him on the bar.

"In her room." Nash took a step back, eager to put some space between him and his furious friend, and noticing then, as he never had before, that whilst Edmund matched him in height and gait, he was a little broader about the shoulders. That would make all the difference, were the two to come to blows. *Blows?* He shook his head. This was Edmund. There would be no resorting to violence.

"In *her* room," Nash reiterated. "We travel as companions, Ed, so do not act rashly -"

"Rashly?" Edmund hissed, glancing over his shoulder to be sure he had not been overheard. "You persuade an impressionable young girl to run away with you and now counsel *me* against acting rashly? Just what did you expect to gain from this?"

"I don't know," Nash blurted, after a long moment of silence, interrupted only by heckling and shouts from the betting corner. Nash shook his head, his eyes blurring with unshed tears as he realised the enormity of the disservice he had done to Louisa. He cared for her, yes, but if he truly loved her, as he claimed, he ought never to have led her into such a misadventure as this. The disappointed backward glance she had offered him as she climbed the stairs to the room he had taken in a falsified name taunted him, then, a reminder of the position he had placed her in.

"Did you even plan to marry her at all?" Edmund asked, raking a hand through his hair and looking older and wearier than Nash could ever recall having seen him before. "What was your goal here? You sought to hurt her, to hurt the Turners?"

"No!" Nash insisted, holding out a placating hand he removed only when Edmund looked as if he might prefer to rip it from his body. He dropped his arm to his side fumbling with his cufflink. "I meant to marry her. I *mean* to. But my aunt...she never would have allowed it. You have met her." He let out a low, bitter laugh. "Could you ever see her giving up her own dreams to allow me to pursue my own?"

"That is no excuse."

"It is not," Nash agreed. "But I felt desperate. She had me married before I had even been given the chance to properly know my fiancée, had shared the good tidings of a de facto engagement before I had ever even posed the question to Miss Carter." Nash swallowed. "I confess, I flirted and played the game with Louisa in the countryside. I was enjoying my liberty, knowing it would come to its end all too soon. That was why I was so reluctant to come back to London. I daresay I outstayed my welcome a little and you were eager to at last be rid of me." He smiled, but Edmund remained stony-faced and silent. "When I saw Louisa again, at the assembly, I realised what I had walked away from and I realised I shouldn't - I couldn't -

live my life without her." He sank his head into his hands. "I saw no other solution than this, but I am - I am sorry, Ed." He lifted his gaze, hoping to see something like forgiveness in his old friend's features.

Edmund did not smile, but his voice softened, almost imperceptibly, and had Nash not known him so long or so well he would have missed the tiniest way his frown relaxed.

"You are a fool, Weston. And you'll not live this down easily." He let out a long sigh. "But I dare say you will live it down eventually. Come, let's fetch Louisa and make for London. It is late, but not so late that travelling this evening is out of the question." He glanced around the inn, barely concealing his disgust with a curl of his lip. "I do not imagine either of you would prefer to remain here when you might be at home."

Home. Nash nodded, for he well saw the wisdom in this plan for Louisa. Louisa would be welcomed back, would have a room ready and waiting for her at her aunt's house. As for *Nash's* aunt...

"She knows, I suppose? My aunt, I mean."

"She is aware that something is amiss." Edmund fixed him with an unflinching look. "I do not know how much she will have pieced together from my enquiry, although I sought to be circumspect. It is lucky I found you here at all, a hunch following a question following a hope."

"I am glad you did," Nash confessed. "It was wrong - I was wrong and I - I am sorry, Ed."

"It is not me you need to apologise to," Edmund said, stiffly. "And I doubt that this is the last apology you'll be forced to make in light of this." He glanced at his watch, then at the darkened windows. "Come, let's not linger any longer. We have quite a journey back and Louisa's family must know she is safe."

He strode past Nash upstairs, barely pausing to enquire what room was hers and Nash, after hesitating a full moment, followed him.

Chapter Sixteen

"Edmund!"

Louisa's evident relief at Edmund's arrival surprised even him, for as soon as she opened the door and saw him there, with Nash in tow, she had thrown herself into his arms, stiffening only as she realised the implication of his arrival.

"Oh." She crept back into the room, chewing listlessly on a fingernail. She appeared to be weighing her response, and after an interminable moment straightened, dropping her hands to her sides and lifting her chin so that she might look him directly in his eyes, a flash of the old imperiousness flaring in her delicate features. "You are here, then."

"I am here," Edmund replied, glancing over his shoulder at Nash, who looked meekly at the floor and said nothing. "I am here to bring you home, Louisa. Gather your belongings. It is already late and we have a long way to travel."

"Nash?" Her voice quavered a little, betraying that her attitude was more affectation than genuine.

"He's right, Lou," Nash said, stepping into the doorway beside Edmund and smiling faintly at her. "The game's up. Let's go home."

Louisa glanced tremulously from one gentleman to the other, before stamping her feet in frustration or disappointment and snatching up the small bundle she had brought with her: her reticule, bonnet and shawl, all that she might have escaped her aunt's house with without drawing undue notice.

"You have no other bags?" Edmund asked, although he already knew what her answer would be. What had they been thinking, to embark on such a journey so ill-equipped? "Very well, come downstairs and I shall see about engaging a carriage."

This would not be an inexpensive acquisition and he drew a breath, thinking it would be the very beginning of what it would cost to put this mistake right. As the trio descended the stairs, Edmund massaged his forehead, where a sharp pain indicated the beginning of a crushing headache. With a sigh, he began to make arrangements with an inn-keeper who was only too eager to be of assistance when enough money was exchanged. Several servants gathered around, whispering and giggling as they observed the crestfallen couple and their weary pursuer, but one glare from Edmund sent them scurrying back to the kitchen.

"You will want to eat before you embark on your dinner, sir. I might set a table -"

The innkeeper's obsequious attention rankled Edmund's already fraying nerves, and a drunken shout from one corner persuaded him against any further delay.

"Alas, no. We shall be on our way."

"Then allow me to pull together some morsels for your journey." The innkeeper clicked his fingers and one of the absent servants reappeared, springing into action. The innkeeper smiled toothily at him. "No extra charge."

"You are very kind," Edmund replied, resisting the urge to roll his eyes. He emptied a coin-purse into his hands and sought through its contents, before offering the whole quantity with a swallowed sigh of resignation. "I trust this will adequately compensate you for your trouble, and the use of your carriage."

"Quite so, sir, quite so!" the innkeeper beamed, delighted at this unexpected bounty.

The door to the inn flew open and a gruff driver entered long enough to nod at the innkeeper and bit his retreat.

"Your carriage is ready, sir. And here -" He turned to the servant, taking the bundle she offered. "Is enough food to see you on your way. Good evening, sir, and travelling mercies!" He made a vague sign with one hand and Edmund dismissed him with a nod, ushering both Nash and Louisa out ahead of him. You would not imagine them lovers to see the careful distance they maintained form each other and from him. Both of their heads were bent, their eyes tracing the floor as they made their way out of the inn and silently boarded the carriage.

This silence remained long after their journey began and Edmund was grateful for it. He had not the temper or energy to endure any list of justifications he could imagine pouring from either Nash or Louisa's lips. Leaning his head against the window he allowed his eyes to close, already imagining the reunion that would await them when their small, weary party arrived in London.

He glanced over at Louisa, who was sitting opposite him, a whole seat to herself. She had curled up like a cat and somehow, miraculously, appeared to be asleep. The day had taken its toll on her. Edmund could not begrudge her that, and leaned forward to tug her shawl a little tighter around her, for though their carriage was warm, the night was chilly.

He leaned back in his seat, catching sight of Nash as he did. His friend looked drawn and exhausted, more weary and worried than he could ever recall seeing him. A smirk tugged at his lips. No doubt Nash, too, feared his reception. *As well he ought!* The man had been idiotic, concocting this scheme and luring Louisa into it and for what? For it all to come crashing down around them before they had even cleared two counties?

"I did not mean it to go like this," Nash said, his voice little more than a whisper. His eyes strayed to Louisa, heavy with regret and affection, even now. "She deserves better than this."

"She does," Edmund agreed. "And are you prepared to do better in future?" He shook his head, marvelling at his friend's self-pity. "You are not a villain, Nash, nor are you cruel. There is a whole life stretching before you and you might yet make good of this."

Nash muttered something in response that Edmund did not immediately hear, and he tilted his head a little closer, silently inviting his friend to repeat the comment.

"You do not know how blessed you are," Nash muttered. "You have fortune enough to live exactly as you choose. Providence has smiled on you. You are lucky."

"I know, Nash. I am well aware of it." He paused, massaging his forehead once more. "I think it is you who are unaware of your own good fortune. If you were, you would not have sought to squander it."

Nash glanced at him, his eyes wide.

"Louisa cares for you. The Turners care for you, as do Mama and I. Why did you not come to us? We might have helped -"

Nash snorted as if the very notion of asking for help was even more ridiculous than the idea he might have received it.

"I suppose there will be no help now," he said, sourly, kicking his heel against the floor of the carriage.

Edmund turned to survey him, his expression weary.

"What do you think this is?"

"THANK GOODNESS YOU'RE alright!"

Mrs Turner threw her arms around Louisa, and Aunt Brierley threw her arms around both of them, awkwardly ushering the pair to a settee that had been moved closer to the hearth, where an unnecessarily warm fire was blazing.

"I have ordered some tea!" Colonel Brierley murmured, wringing his hands and trotting after the trio with an evident desire to be helpful.

"Thank you, Edmund." Mr Turner looked older than his years, having aged considerably in a day. He grasped Edmund's hand in both of his and smiled, at last releasing it and leaning rather heavily on his cane as he, too, made his way into the parlour.

"Yes, thank you," Juliet said, sliding close enough to Edmund to kiss him and nestle her arm through his. She peered over his shoulder to where Nash stood, uncomfortably, at the threshold, and steered Edmund after her family.

"I had better not stop," Edmund whispered, freeing himself gently from her grasp. "Nash is dead on his feet and has a hellish reception waiting for him at his aunt's house."

"As if he deserves any less!" Juliet retorted, her eyes flashing angrily. When Edmund did not immediately agree with her, she transferred some of her anger to him. "You cannot say that you feel sorry for him! After all that he did?"

Edmund shrugged, rubbing the back of his neck wearily. When he spoke, though, he was quick to appease his fiery fiancée, who turned away, poise to abandon him in defiance.

"Of course I do not approve of what happened," he said, tilting Juliet's chin up so she would look at him again. He kissed her softly and smiled. "I certainly wish they had gone about it a different way, but I cannot put all the blame on him. Louisa might have refused."

"Louisa is young -"

"Louisa knows her mind, not unlike her sister." Edmund's smile grew. "Tell me, have you ever managed to persuade her to do anything she did not wish to do? Or, contrary to that, persuade her out of her desired course?"

Juliet frowned but was unable to contradict this.

"I still lay the blame for this at *his* feet." She would not grace Mr Weston with his name, fearing that it would burn her lips when she uttered it, so furious was he with the trouble he had caused.

"He blames himself, too," Edmund cajoled. "And he shall have to bear the consequences of his actions, do not fret." His voice grew serious. "I feel quite sure his aunt will disown him after this. You know his family is not rich, and she has been the source of all his income and support." He sighed. "It will be a hard road for him to walk alone, and he shall have a great deal of penance to do before she may countenance seeing him again."

"Good," Juliet said, folding her arms stubbornly. She looked at Edmund. "You'll not persuade me to feel sorry for him, Ed, so you might as well stop trying now."

"Very well." Edmund's eyes twinkled and he pressed a kiss to her forehead. "You may be angry at him this evening. I shall take him home with me, I think, where he may be guaranteed of admission past the front door. And tomorrow..." he sighed, rumpling his hair even more than it already was. "We shall see. Things always look brighter in the morning."

Juliet sniffed, not quite willing or able to give credence to this simple-minded view of things, but she did embrace Edmund as he turned to go, and whispered her own, heartfelt thanks for all he had done in rescuing her sister.

"Don't blame Nash for everything," Edmund whispered. "Or Louisa. We've all acted a little rash where love was concerned." He winked and Juliet punched him lightly on the arm so that their romantic parting ended in muffled laughter, and Juliet still wore the ghost of a smile as she retraced her steps back into the parlour.

"Has Edmund gone?" Colonel Brierley asked, hovering awkwardly in one corner, holding a pipe he did not smoke and brandishing a glass carafe, ready to fill any glasses he could find.

"He has," Juliet said. "With Mr Weston."

Aunt Brierley seemed somehow gifted with supernatural hearing, because her head darted up at this, her eyes narrowing in suspicion.

"And well he might disappear from this house!" she hissed. "Dreadful man!"

"Sister," Mr Turner began, his forehead creasing.

"You mustn't speak of him so!" Louisa wailed, looking up from her mother's face to her aunt's. "We love one another, Aunt, and we shall be married. You'll see."

"Marry? Ha!"

"Let's not speak of it any more tonight," Mrs Turner said, smoothing Louisa's hair and shooting her sister-in-law a warning look. "There will be time enough for all of that tomorrow. It's late."

Late it was, and everyone was exhausted, but nobody seemed willing to leave the comforts of the parlour, so they fell into a kind of stupor, making vague, murmured conversation and merely enjoying the comforts of being all together until the first rays of sunlight dawned.

Chapter Seventeen

Nash had shrugged off Edmund's support on the morning he went to call on his aunt. In truth, he might have valued some sort of moral support, but he was not sure whether having his friend beside him would help or hinder his case. He drew in a breath, his heart-rate quickening with every step he took along the familiar street to his aunt's elegant townhouse. Edmund had relented, allowing him to go alone but promising to meet him at the club later to debrief. Nash had bargained him down from the club to the White Lion, an anonymous inn where the pair might avoid being seen by others in their set. Nash was not sure he could face meeting Finch or Heatherington or Gill straight away after surviving the reunion with his aunt.

He had reached the door, now, and raised his hand to knock, waiting a moment before he did so. He had an overwhelming urge to flee, but fought it, knowing that the ordeal would become no less enjoyable the longer he delayed it. Screwing closed his eyes, he rapped three times sharply on the door and was shown up to his aunt's room, little surprised to see her still in bed and determined to see him nonetheless.

"Would you prefer me to come back later, Auntie?" he asked, from the doorway to her elegant room.

"I would not." Her voice was little more than a bark, and brooked no disobedience, so Nash took a tentative step forward.

"You look well," he began, biting his lip.

"No more do you," she replied. "But I suppose I cannot expect any more than that when you have been on an adventure overnight." She looked past him to a servant, silently ordering them to close the door and disappear, avoiding any chance of their being overheard.

"What were you thinking, running away with that Turner girl?" she exploded. "You do it to try me, I suppose, to test my patience and my affection." She sniffed, noisily. "It will not work. You are fortunate I permit you entrance to my house at all after that little scheme!"

"Aunt -"

"Abigail knows nothing about it, yet," she continued, in a low whisper. "I was fortunate enough to keep the knowledge from her, but she will hear of it in time. I suggest you disappear and allow time to take its effect, rather than jilting her personally, unless you wish to cause her still more pain."

Nash shook his head, feeling a flash of remorse that he might wound the cousin who had done nothing but be controlled by his aunt, as he had been.

"She will find a better class of suitor, you may rest assured of that. I shall see to it." His aunt flicked a reproachful glance towards him. "I must say I am disappointed, Nash. I thought you a great many things, but foolish was not amongst them. Well, I dare say you shall recover in time. It is always young ladies who suffer more in these situations." A flash of interest flickered across her face. "Where will you go? The continent? You might join the regiment and make a name for yourself."

"I have not yet decided," Nash began, fumbling with his cuff.

"The clergy won't have you," she said, scornfully. "And you can forget any thought of inheritance after this little performance. One task I asked of you, one that would ensure the future happiness of our family and you have thrown my generosity away. I am pleased to know what you think of my name, as well as my money." Leaning across her bed, she snatched up a bell, ringing it noisily. "You may leave me, now. I shall look for your letter at Christmas."

Firmly dismissed, Nash allowed his aunt's servant to escort him to his guest room and gathered his few belongings, pausing at the table he had used as a desk and penning a quick note to his cousin, full of vague explanation and light on detail, suggesting he would be gone quite some time and wishing her well. It would work better if his aunt had not declared to all and sundry that they were engaged, but he did put some faith in her ability to rectify the situation. She would focus all her energies, now, in ensuring Abigail met someone new, and as soon as he had the word of her engagement, he would be free to pursue his own. In the meantime, he must seek to make something of himself. *You might join the regiment...* That was something he could do. And he had always so admired the dashing red of their uniforms. How well he would look.

Somewhat cheered by this mental picture, he even managed to whistle as he walked the long and winding path to the White Lion, finding Edmund skulking in a darkened corner, nursing a drink and laying out a game of patience with a languid air.

"You survived, then?" he murmured, as Nash sidled up to join him.

Nash said nothing but reached across him to make a move he had missed.

"What now?" Edmund muttered, nodding an acquiescence of the move, which bought him a few minutes longer of a game.

"I am homeless," Nash declared, leaning back in his chair and feeling surprisingly unworried by this turn of events. If anything, he felt free. Free of the burden of his aunt's expectations, free of all obligations...all except one, that is. "I must speak to Louisa, and to her father."

Edmund lifted his gaze, looking carefully at Nash as if seeing to the very depths of his being.

"You mean to marry her, then?"

"Of course I mean to marry her." Nash was affronted. "I would not have acted so rashly if I did not care for her." He winced. "I confess, it was rash in the extreme and certainly did not turn out at all as I supposed, but now...now we may have our time over, and do it properly this time."

He drummed a rhythm on the table.

"And I wonder if I might trouble you for an introduction. You are a little acquainted with Colonel Black, I believe? Is he recruiting at present, do you know?"

LOUISA'S VISIT TO LONDON had not ended at all how she imagined, but not as terribly as it might have, either. Their journey home to Aston House had nothing of the merriment of their journey *from* it, although there was a sense of peace and calm that even she could not baulk at. Her future was ascertained, not in the way she had dreamed it would be, but in a way that would lead, she hoped, to future happiness.

Colonel Weston. She smiled, sinking a little further back into her seat in the carriage. It was a little way off yet, of course. Nash had to earn his rank, but he was quite determined. He had said as much when he called, contrite and cautious, to speak with Mr Turner that morning. Their interview had been long, but both men had emerged unscathed, and even shook hands, before sharing their plan with the women who were crowded in the parlour, eager to be told what would happen.

I am engaged, and even though my wedding is some time away yet, I may rest content in the hope of its existence! Louisa told herself, recalling the shy, stumbling way Nash had told her of his hopes to secure a position within the regiment and, with Edmund's help, to succeed in securing both rank and fortune enough to make a comfortable future for them. He would look so becoming in his regimentals, Mrs Turner had said, with a warmth and encouragement that far outshone Juliet. Louisa glanced at her sister, who was frowning sternly at the countryside they passed. She had not been so quick to forgive Nash, nor to pardon her sister's part in their foolishness, although Louisa dared to hope that in time she might soften. Edmund would help with that, too.

Louisa's smile faltered as she thought of how much she owed to dear Edmund. He had truly done all that was in his power, and far more than he was obliged to, to help settle the matter between Nash and her. It was his word and his wealth that smoothed the way for Nash to progress and create his fortune, and his support that helped sway Mr Turner to consent to the match. *Papa would do whatever would make me happy*, Louisa thought, but she had noticed the sadness that lingered in her father's features, the way his smile did not quite reach his eyes. It had not been a conventional plan, nor a conventional match, but then Louisa Turner was not a conventional young lady. She still saw nothing but romance in the way Nash had thrown aside his future for her, and could not fault his commitment in his willingness to wait and work for their life together. Their marriage was agreed, yes, but it was not to take place for at least a year or two, yet. This, Louisa was not entirely happy about, but she considered it a sensible compromise, and thus she complied with only minimal complaint.

"We shall invite Maddy and Robert to dine with us this evening, I think, my dear," Mrs Turner murmured, folding her hand over her husband's, and speaking in a voice designed to reach only his ears. Louisa straightened, intent on hearing, whilst not seeming to listen.

"Bess will come with them, of course, and we may share Louisa's news then. Do you think it worth waiting until Christopher can join us?"

Mr Turner's eyelids flickered behind his spectacles.

"He is busy with concerts all this week! No, I think we shall proceed as you suggest. A small family dinner this evening will be the very best for breaking the news. Christopher will hear of it in time..."

Louisa frowned, a little unsettled to hear the weary tone in her father's voice. She forgot to feign ignorance, then, her eyes sliding over to him, and he met her gaze for the briefest instant before relaxing into a smile designed to put her mind at ease.

"What do you think, Louisa? Will your sisters not be surprised to hear your news?"

"Surprised, yes." Louisa nodded, swallowing her concern. "And pleased! They are fond of Nash and will be only too happy to call him brother, I am sure!"

Juliet harrumphed from her corner of the carriage but when Louisa looked at her, her gaze was still fixed on the window, so she was left to conclude she imagined the sound, or that it related to some secret thought in Juliet's head.

"Perhaps, when Nash is a situated in the barracks, we shall have him to dine too," Mrs Turner suggested, with a genial smile. "After all, we have already grown rather used to him being a regular visitor at Aston House. I do not suppose that will change, now."

"Indeed, not!" Louisa declared, beaming at her mother. "If anything, he will come more often, not less. I think he will make a fine addition..."

She launched into a detailed description of all the delightful visits she had planned for her new fiancé on the days he was not pledged to work with the regiment. It would scarcely be any different than before, except now she and Nash would be able to freely plan their future. And one day, when he had earned enough of rank and fortune to take his own property, she and Nash could embark on their own life together.

With a sigh, she snuggled back into the corner of the carriage, allowing her eyelids to grow heavy as she dreamed about the elegant home they would make, and how envious all her sisters would be of her thrilling, regimental romance...

Epilogue

"How charming the house looks decorated just so!"

"Indeed, yes...it is charming, but - my dear - please do not stand there admiring it! You are obstructing the doorway!"

Maddy laughed as she steered her hapless husband out of the way of arriving guests, and settled him comfortably in a seat next to his father, while she slipped upstairs to check on Juliet.

"Maddy! Oh, thank heavens for some sanity!" Juliet cried, when the door to her dressing room opened to admit the last Turner sister.

"Rude!" Louisa shrieked, turning her sister's head back to face the mirror. "Now stop fidgeting and let us work."

"Poor Juliet, how we are all hanging over you to make you perfect...and how you hate us for it!" Bess sang, smoothing an invisible crease from the pretty jade green dress Juliet had selected for a bridal gown.

"It's quite unnecessary," Juliet said, obediently keeping her head very still while Louisa tended to her hair. "Everybody here has seen me and knows what I look like. It is a farce to try and make me a fashion-plate."

"You do want to look well on your wedding day, though, don't you, dear?" Mrs Turner asked. She was perched on the bed, watching her daughters and surreptitiously dabbing at her eyes with a handkerchief when sentiment overwhelmed her.

"I want to look like *myself*. Poor Edmund will not recognise me!"

At last, she could bear it no more and batted her younger sisters away before one last glance in the mirror pronounced her acceptable. Turning to greet Maddy properly, she smiled.

"Well?"

"Beautiful!" Maddy agreed. "And quite like yourself."

"Just think, Juliet, you might look like this every day if only you took a little time and care," Louisa observed, entirely ignorant of the sharp look of censure she received in retaliation from her older sister.

"Well, Bess, come along and let's find our seats. I want to be close enough to see Edmund's face when he lays eyes on you!" Grinning, she took Bess by the hand and the two young ladies scurried off, leaving Juliet, Maddy and her mother to make the final touches before following them downstairs to join everyone in the grand room where the wedding would take place.

"It scarcely looks like Northridge Place at all!" Mrs Turner said, admiring the clutches of flowers placed here and there and ordained with ribbons.

"Yes, Mrs Gale has such an eye for decoration," Juliet agreed, with a grin. "It is fortunate, for I am terrible at it, and if we are to host dinners and balls and all manner of celebrations here, I shall have to learn." She pulled a face, and her mother and sister laughed.

Maddy glanced over her shoulder, seeing her seat still empty beside her husband, and offered her sister one last embrace before hurrying off to join him. Mrs Turner, too, squeezed Juliet warmly before handing her off to her husband and finding her seat in the crowd of friends and family who had all been invited to share in the happy day.

"Well, Juliet!" Mr Turner said, smiling at her as they took their places at one end of a long aisle that led the way along the room to where Edmund and Reverend Worthy awaited them. "Are you ready?"

"Yes," Juliet said, her eyes fixing on the uncharacteristically neat head of her husband-to-be and smiling. They had waited a long time to reach this point, she and Edmund. She had seen two other sisters married: Maddy and Robert, sitting contentedly together with his father who had become like a second Papa to all of the Turner girls and was adored by them all; and Bess and Christopher, who sat alongside his sister, who had promised, along with her brother, to provide all the music required at the celebration and leave Bess free simply to enjoy herself. Even Louisa was engaged, although she sat with friends, clutching the note that Nash had written that morning, apologising for his absence, but wishing every happiness to the couple that had become his closest friends and supporters as he continued to work hard and excel in his career. Their wedding would come soon, Juliet knew, but was still some time away yet.

"What a year it has been, Papa," she murmured, as they began their slow progress down the aisle. "How quickly it seems to have flown by, and yet how long it has taken to reach this point."

Edmund turned, then, catching sight of Juliet for the first time that day, and his entire face erupted in a smile that she could not help but return.

"Dearly beloved..."

Reverend Worthy began the familiar verse, and the entire room hushed to listen, as Juliet and Edmund made their first vows to one another as husband and wife, and another happy union was begun.

The End

About the Author

Meg Osborne[2] is an avid reader, tea drinker and unrepentant history nerd. She writes sweet historical romance stories and Jane Austen fanfiction, and can usually be found knitting, dreaming up new stories, or on twitter @megoswrites[3]

For updates and new release news – and for a free book! – sign up to Meg's newsletter list here[4]

---

1. https://megosbornewrites.com/

2. https://megosbornewrites.com/

3. https://twitter.com/megoswrites

4. https://dl.bookfunnel.com/1q3ks9bpku

5. https://dl.bookfunnel.com/1q3ks9bpku

Ingram Content Group UK Ltd.
Milton Keynes UK
UKHW040728260623
424053UK00001B/16